**PUPPY PATROL** ™

# LOST AND FOUND

# BOOKS IN THE PUPPY PATROL SERIES ™

1. TEACHER'S PET
2. BIG BEN
3. ABANDONED!
4. DOUBLE TROUBLE
5. STAR PAWS
6. TUG OF LOVE
7. SAVING SKYE
8. TUFF'S LUCK
9. RED ALERT
10. THE GREAT ESCAPE
11. PERFECT PUPPY
12. SAM AND DELILAH
13. THE SEA DOG
14. PUPPY SCHOOL
15. A WINTER'S TALE
16. PUPPY LOVE
17. BEST OF FRIENDS
18. KING OF THE CASTLE
19. POSH PUP
20. CHARLIE'S CHOICE

21. THE PUPPY PROJECT
22. SUPERDOG!
23. SHERLOCK'S HOME
24. FOREVER SAM
25. MILLY'S TRIUMPH
26. THE SNOW DOG
27. BOOMERANG BOB
28. WILLOW'S WOODS
29. DOGNAPPED!
30. PUPPY POWER!
31. TWO'S COMPANY
32. DIGGER'S TREASURE
33. HOMEWARD BOUND
34. THE PUPPY EXPRESS
35. ORPHAN PUPPY
36. BARNEY'S RESCUE
37. LOST AND FOUND

## COMING SOON!

38. TOP DOG!

TM

# LOST AND FOUND

## JENNY DALE

Illustrations by Mick Reid
Cover illustration by Michael Rowe

---

AN
**APPLE**
PAPERBACK

---

SCHOLASTIC INC.
New York  Toronto  London  Auckland  Sydney
Mexico City  New Delhi  Hong Kong  Buenos Aires

SPECIAL THANKS TO NARINDER DHAMI

No part of this publication may be reproduced, in whole or in part, or stored in a retrieval system, or transmitted in any form or by any means, electronic, mechanical, photocopying, recording, or otherwise, without the written permission of the publisher. For information regarding permission, please write to Macmillan Publishers Ltd., 20 New Wharf Rd., London N1 9RR Basingstoke and Oxford.

ISBN 0-439-54359-2

12 11 10 9 8 7 6 5 4 3 2        3 4 5 6 7 8/0

Printed in the U.S.A.
First Scholastic printing, September 2003

**CHAPTER ONE**

"**C**areful, Jake!" Neil Parker took a deep breath as he watched his young black-and-white Border collie balancing on the center of the makeshift seesaw. As the seesaw tilted, Jake ran lightly down to the other end of the plank and jumped off.

"Good boy, Jake!" Neil shouted proudly. He was training Jake to take part in his very first agility competition, which was about three weeks away. The seesaw was one of the most difficult obstacles for dogs to master. If they jumped off before they reached the end, they received penalty points. Neil and Jake had been working on it for the last half hour, and the young dog had finally gotten the hang of it.

Jake was obviously thrilled with himself. He

1

bounded across the barn to Neil, tongue lolling and feathery tail wagging furiously, and gave a loud bark as if to say, "Didn't I do well!"

Neil felt in his pocket for a couple of the dog treats he always carried, and Jake wolfed them down eagerly. "You're doing just fine, Jake," Neil told him, ruffling the young dog's thick fur affectionately. "You'll be as good as your dad one day."

A lump rose in Neil's throat as he thought about his first dog, Sam, who was Jake's father. Sam's weak heart meant that he'd had to retire from competing when he was young. Neil had had to look after him carefully, feeding him a special diet and making sure Sam didn't tire himself out. But the collie had died after rescuing Jake from a flooded river. Not a day went by without Neil thinking of him.

Neil lived and breathed dogs. At eleven, he already knew exactly what he wanted to do when he grew up. He was going to work with dogs, just like his parents. Bob and Carole Parker ran King Street Kennels — a boarding kennel and rescue center in the country town of Compton. Neil couldn't imagine living anywhere else. He loved being surrounded by dogs.

Neil ran a hand through his spiky brown hair and blinked hard as a strong ray of sunlight suddenly slanted through the windows of Red's Barn. "Looks like it's stopped raining, boy," he remarked, throwing Jake another treat. "Come on, let's go through the course one more time." Usually, Neil set up the course in the exercise field next to the kennel, but today the rain had been too heavy to practice outside, so they'd come indoors instead.

Neil led his dog to the start of the obstacle course. He'd built it from various planks, bricks, ropes, and other bits and pieces he'd found lying around.

As he signaled to Jake to begin, Neil could hear cars pulling up outside. Saturday was always a busy day for visitors at King Street Kennels. Weekly boarders arrived with their owners, and people came to look at the dogs who were up for adoption. The

rescue center was quite full at the moment, and Neil hoped that at least one or two of the dogs would find new homes today.

"Jake!" Neil groaned suddenly. Instead of running through the old tire that Neil had propped upright with a couple of bricks, the Border collie had run around it.

"No, Jake!" Neil said sternly, leading him back to do it again. This time, Jake did it correctly, and Neil rewarded him with a dog treat.

"Jake looks like he's doing well!" a voice called from the barn doorway. Neil turned around to see his ten-year-old sister Emily watching them.

"He's doing OK," he replied with a grin. "But sometimes he gets a bit excited and forgets what he's supposed to do!"

"I bet you'll win the agility competition, Jake," Emily told the young dog, who had trotted over to be stroked. Jake wagged his tail hard as if he completely agreed with her.

"Does Dad need a hand?" Neil asked, beginning to clear away the obstacle course. He loved helping out in the kennel when he could, although school often got in the way.

"Well, there are quite a few visitors at the rescue center, but Mom's there looking after them," Emily replied. "And Dad's with Mike." Mike Turner was the local vet who came to King Street Kennels every Saturday morning to run a dog clinic. "But guess what?" Emily went on. "The Morrises have just arrived at Old Mill Farm."

"Oh yeah?" Neil was immediately interested. Old Mill Farm bordered the exercise field, so the people who lived there were the Parkers' nearest neighbors. The previous owners, Jane and Richard, had recently moved to the United States, following a fire at the farm. They had taken their Border collie Delilah, who was Jake's mom, with them. The beautiful house, a converted water mill, had been gutted by the fire, but the Hammonds had still managed to find a buyer. Jane Hammond had told the Parkers that a couple by the name of Graham and Jo Morris and their two children would be moving in.

"I thought we could go over and say hello." Emily hurried to help Neil lift one of the heavy planks of wood.

"You thought we could go and have a look around, you mean?" Neil teased her.

"Well, they are our neighbors," protested Emily. "And I'm only being friendly!"

"OK," Neil agreed. "But we'd better tell Mom and Dad where we're going."

Secretly, he was just as curious as Emily about their new neighbors. The Parkers often used the public footpath that crossed Old Mill Farm to walk the dogs, so they'd be bumping into the Morris family all the time. It was probably a good idea to get to know them.

Neil whistled to Jake, who immediately bounded

over, and the three of them headed out of the barn
into the courtyard at the back of the Parkers' house.
The kennel blocks ran along two sides of the courtyard, and housed the dogs who were boarding at
King Street.

"Look, there they are." Emily pointed across the
exercise field. The blackened ruins of the converted
water mill could be seen in the distance, and Neil
could just about make out a car parked outside with
a trailer hitched to the back of it. "Jane and the Morrises are going to live in the trailer while they fix up
the house."

"It needs a *lot* of fixing up!" Neil said. The house
was a complete mess, and all because some tourists
had accidentally started a fire in the woods up on the
nearby hill. Neil still got angry when he thought
about how many lives had been put at risk by such
carelessness.

"Jane said that Mr. Morris is a writer and Mrs.
Morris is a dentist," Emily remarked as they headed
toward the rescue center to see their mother. "Imagine being a dentist! I wouldn't want to go around
sticking my fingers into other people's mouths."

"Yeah, lots of people hate dentists, don't they?"
Neil said.

"Especially Sarah!" Emily pointed out, and they
both laughed. The last time their five-year-old sister
had been taken to the dentist she had refused to

open her mouth, despite all their mother's threats and bribes.

At that moment, Sarah hurtled out of the rescue center at top speed. Neil caught her just before she crashed right into him.

"Calm down, Squirt," he said, laughing. "You'll frighten the dogs!"

"Guess what? We're going to Disney World!" Sarah said breathlessly.

Neil and Emily looked at each other.

"You're not still talking about that, are you, Sarah?" Emily sighed. Ever since their parents had mentioned that they should start thinking about where to go for their summer vacation, Sarah had been begging and pleading for a trip to Disney World in Florida. Neil and Emily didn't think she had much hope of getting it, although Bob and Carole Parker hadn't exactly said no yet.

"Well, I was in the rescue center with Mom just now, and she said she'd think about it!" Sarah said triumphantly, then ran off toward the house. "I've got to tell Fudge!" Sarah's hamster Fudge was her pride and joy.

Emily nudged Neil. "Mom probably just said that to get rid of her," she said.

Neil agreed with her. *Mom must be busy today with all the visitors,* he thought as he stepped aside to allow yet another family into the rescue center.

Now that the rain had stopped and the sun was shining, most of the dogs were bounding around in their outside runs, looking happy, healthy, and lively. Neil was sure that at least one of them would find a loving new home today.

"Should I go in and find Mom—?" Emily began, when suddenly a voice from behind them called their names.

Neil and Emily spun around to see Bev Mitchell, one of King Street's hardworking kennel assistants, hurrying across the courtyard toward them. Trotting along beside her was a dog Neil had never seen before.

"Neil!" Emily nudged him again. *"Look!"*

It was the strangest-looking dog Neil had ever seen. He was mostly white with patches of black. He had a large head, a short, tubby body, and stumpy legs that looked too small to hold him up. He also had a large patch of black over one eye, which made him look . . . like a pirate.

"Hi, you two!" Bev smiled at Neil and Emily as they hurried over to her. "Meet Pirate."

"Great name!" Neil laughed as he bent down to greet the dog. "Hello, Pirate."

Pirate's stump of a tail began to wag furiously. He sniffed Neil's hand and then gently licked it, pressing his sturdy body against Neil's legs and obviously enjoying all the attention.

"Oh, he's cute!" Emily exclaimed, fondling the dog's

funny little floppy ears. Pirate immediately rolled over onto his back and waggled his legs in the air, a blissful look on his face.

"He's a cutie, all right," Bev agreed. "Even though he's not going to win any beauty contests!"

"Is he a boarder?" Neil asked with a frown. He always kept an eye on the dogs coming and going from King Street Kennels, and he didn't remember seeing Pirate's name on any paperwork.

"No, he's been admitted to the rescue center," Bev replied. "We got the call only a half hour ago. His elderly owner died earlier this week, and her son wanted to get rid of Pirate. He said that if we didn't go pick him up immediately, he'd have him put to sleep, so Bob sent me off in the Range Rover to get him."

"What a horrible man!" Emily said indignantly, and Neil nodded in agreement.

"Well, let's hope this doggy finds a new home quickly," Bev said, scratching the top of Pirate's head. "I'm sure someone will realize what a great dog he is, even if he does look a bit funny!"

Just then, another family crossed the courtyard and headed toward the rescue center.

"Hey, look at that weird dog," said the oldest boy, pointing at Pirate. He burst out laughing, and so did the rest of the family. "He looks like something out of a cartoon!"

Pirate looked scared. Whimpering a little, he hid behind Emily's legs, ears down. Neil glared at the family as they went into the rescue center, still laughing.

"Ignore them, boy," he whispered. "You're a great dog!"

"We'd better put Pirate on the King Street Kennels web site." Emily suggested as Pirate licked Neil's hand gratefully. "He could be our Dog of the Week."

"Good idea," Neil agreed, just as their father and Mike Turner emerged from the dog clinic.

"Ah, this must be Pirate," Bob Parker said with a smile. He was a tall, broad-shouldered man with brown hair and a short, thick beard. "Any problems, Bev?"

Bev shook her head as Bob squatted down and gently stroked Pirate's back.

"No, Pirate's vaccinations are up-to-date. I've got all the paperwork."

"I'll check him over, just in case," Mike said cheerfully. "He's a bit of a mix, isn't he? Looks like there's some bull terrier in there, along with several other breeds!"

"He's a sweet dog, though," Neil said quickly. He felt protective of Pirate already, and was determined to make sure the dog found a good home with owners who would really appreciate him.

"Dad, can we go over to Old Mill Farm?" Emily asked as Bev led Pirate over to the clinic, followed by Mike. "The Morrises have arrived and we want to say hello."

"All right, but don't get in the way," Bob warned them.

"We won't," Neil promised, and he and Emily headed for the exercise field with Jake at their heels.

"You know, maybe Sarah's idea of going to Disney World isn't such a bad one after all," Emily said thoughtfully as they crossed the field. Jake had already run on ahead and was waiting by the gate that led onto the Old Mill Farm land, sniffing around in the long grass.

"What do you mean?" Neil asked.

"Well, if we went to America for our summer vacation, maybe we could go to New York, too, and visit the Hammonds and Delilah," Emily pointed out eagerly.

Neil grinned. "No way, Em! Do you know how far New York is from Florida?"

"No, how far is it?"

"Um . . ." Neil wasn't exactly sure. "Really far. It's miles and miles."

"And we could also go and see Max and Prince in Hollywood," Emily went on, getting carried away with the idea. Max Hooper and his spaniel Prince, stars of the popular TV program *Time Travelers*, were good friends of the Parkers. They were making a film in Hollywood at the moment.

Neil burst out laughing. "Hollywood's in Los Angeles, California, and that's miles from Florida *and* New York! Somehow, I don't think Mom and Dad would be up for it."

"I'm going to ask them anyway," Emily said, unlatching the gate. She had a determined look on her face that Neil knew well, so he decided not to say anything more. After all, Neil would love to go to America. He wasn't too psyched about Disney World, but visiting New York and seeing Delilah again, or Max and Prince in Los Angeles, would be amazing.

Jake was the first one through the gate and dashed off along the public footpath, his feathery tail waving

wildly. Neil and Emily followed at a more leisurely pace.

"Look, there they are," Emily said in a low voice to Neil as they got closer to the farmhouse.

A tall man in jeans and a T-shirt and a slim, blond-haired woman were unloading boxes from the trunk of their car. Two blond children, a girl of about eleven and a boy of around nine, were sitting on the trailer steps. "Let's go and say hello," said Neil.

Neil and Emily headed toward them. But before they could say anything, Mrs. Morris suddenly looked around and spotted Jake, who was bounding along in front. Neil was close enough to see her face change from a smile to a look of absolute fury.

"Is that your dog?" Mrs. Morris shouted, shading her eyes and glaring at Neil and Emily. "Put his leash on — *right now*!"

# CHAPTER TWO

Neil was completely taken aback by the anger in Mrs. Morris's voice. He glanced at Emily, who looked equally stunned, then called, "Jake! Here, boy!"

Jake was already rushing toward the Morris family to say hello, but at the sound of Neil's voice he immediately stopped, wheeled around, and trotted obediently back toward his owner. Fuming inwardly, Neil clipped the leash onto the young dog's collar. What was the matter with Mrs. Morris? Jake was only trying to be friendly.

Meanwhile, Mr. Morris and the two children were looking pretty embarrassed, but none of them said anything. Emily was uncharacteristically silent, and Neil was speechless. They hadn't gotten off to a very good start with their new neighbors.

"Thank you," Mrs. Morris said, breathing hard through her nose as if she was trying to calm herself down. "Now, what can we do for you?"

"We just came to say hello," Neil said, trying not to sound annoyed. "We're Neil and Emily Parker, your new neighbors. We live at King Street Kennels."

"Oh, yes, the *kennel*," Mrs. Morris muttered as if it was somehow a bad word. Then she made an obvious effort to be more polite, and even managed a smile. "Well, I'm Jo Morris, this is my husband Graham, and this is Vicky and that's Tom."

Graham, Vicky, and Tom Morris also smiled at Neil and Emily, but Neil didn't feel like smiling back. Not after the way Jo Morris had spoken to them at first.

"Well, it's very nice to meet you," Jo went on, still trying to be friendly. "But we'll have to ask you to keep your dog away from our land in the future, won't we, Graham?" She turned to her husband and raised her eyebrows at him. 'We really can't have dogs wandering loose all over Old Mill Farm."

"Yes, that's right," her husband agreed, although he still looked uncomfortable.

Neil could hardly believe his ears. "But there's a public footpath through here, even though it's Old Mill Farm land!" he protested.

"Oh, *you're* welcome to use the footpath," Jo Morris said quickly. "We just don't want any dogs on our land."

"Lots of people walk their dogs along this path," Emily said stubbornly.

"Well, we'll have to see about that," Jo Morris said calmly, looking as if she was struggling to keep her temper under control again.

Meanwhile, Neil noticed that Vicky and Tom Morris, who hadn't said a word so far, were looking longingly at Jake.

"Your dog's great," said Tom suddenly. "Can I pet him?"

"Of course —" Neil started to say. But he didn't get a chance.

"Stay where you are, Tom!" Jo Morris ordered her son quickly. "You know I don't like you touching strange dogs."

*Jake's not strange,* Neil thought angrily. *Not as strange as you are, anyway!* He kept quiet with difficulty.

Jo Morris turned to her husband. "I knew it was a mistake to move next door to a kennel," Neil heard her mutter under her breath. "Even if the house *was* very cheap."

"It'll be all right," Graham reassured her, slipping his arm around her waist.

"Come on, Em, let's get out of here," Neil said in a low voice. Emily nodded, and the two of them turned away.

"Bye," Vicky and Tom called after them. Emily

looked around and waved, but Neil was too angry even to do that.

"What was that Jo Morris talking about!" he spluttered as they walked quickly back to the exercise field. "She can't stop people walking their dogs on a public footpath!"

"Well, she seems to think she can," Emily pointed out. "I wonder why she was so unfriendly?"

"It's obvious, isn't it?" Neil said. "Jo Morris just doesn't like dogs! Well, if she thinks she can keep us and the dogs off the footpath, she can think again. . . ."

"And when I told Jo Morris it was a public footpath, she said we were welcome to use it, but not if we had dogs with us!" Neil told his parents indignantly as he sat in the kitchen that evening. He was so wound up that he'd hardly touched his dinner.

"Really?" Carole Parker, tall and dark-haired, turned around from the kitchen counter where she was buttering bread. "That doesn't sound very friendly."

"It does worry me a little," Bob said thoughtfully, sipping his tea. "We use that footpath a lot for walking the dogs. Are you sure you're not exaggerating, Neil?"

Neil shook his head. "That's exactly what she said, isn't it, Em?" he appealed to his sister.

Emily nodded.

"Well, she doesn't have a leg to stand on," Carole

said angrily, slapping a plate of bread and butter down on the table. "That's a public footpath, and Jo Morris can't stop us from walking a hundred dogs on it if we want to!"

"That'd show her, Mom!" Neil grinned at the thought of the Parker family walking one hundred dogs along the Old Mill Farm footpath.

"Let's not get involved in an argument with the Morrises right away," Bob said calmly, making a visible effort to control his own annoyance. "Give them a chance to get settled, and then perhaps they might be more friendly."

"Well, I think they sound horrible!" Sarah put in.

Carole sighed. "Your dad's got a point. Maybe Jo Morris is a bit stressed out, what with having to live in a trailer while they renovate the house. It can't be easy."

"If we went to Disney World, we wouldn't have to see the Morrises," Sarah said hopefully, but everyone ignored her.

"I know what I'll do," Carole said. "I'll stop by with a homemade cake tomorrow morning and say hello."

"Good idea," Bob agreed. "And, in the meantime, it might be a good idea to walk the dogs somewhere else." He looked at Neil and Emily sternly. "OK?"

"OK," Neil agreed reluctantly. He didn't want to give in to Jo Morris, but his dad was right. Maybe it was best to give the family time to settle in.

"We're going to take some photos of Pirate so that

we can put him on the King Street Kennels web site," Emily said as she finished eating. "We thought we'd make him Dog of the Week."

"That's a good idea," Carole said approvingly. "I'm afraid it may not be easy to find him a new home. Most of the visitors commented on how funny he looked!"

Neil's heart sank. "But he's a great dog!"

"I know," Carole agreed. "He's very gentle and loving, and he'd be a wonderful pet."

"And Mike Turner said he's very healthy," Bob added. "But there's no getting away from the fact that Pirate's kind of strange-looking, and that can put off potential owners."

"Em and I will find him a good home," Neil assured his dad as Emily grabbed her camera from the kitchen counter and the two of them left the kitchen. They crossed the courtyard and went over to the rescue center.

"Do you really think Jo Morris will change her mind?" Emily asked.

Neil shrugged. "I don't know. But that won't stop us using the footpath, will it?" He grinned at Emily.

"No way!" Emily agreed determinedly as they walked past the pens to find Pirate.

The mongrel was lying in his basket in a corner of the pen, looking a little glum.

"He probably misses his owner," Neil said.

But Pirate brightened up when he saw them. He

waddled over on his stubby legs and stood there wagging his tail as Neil unlocked the door. Then he waited patiently for them to pet him, sniffing happily at their fingers with his wet, black nose.

"He's so gentle, isn't he?" Emily said. "He'd be perfect for a family with young children, or for an old person."

"Yeah," Neil agreed. "So we've just got to make sure everyone realizes what a great dog he is. Come on, boy." He led Pirate back to his basket. "Sit down so that Em can take your picture."

Pirate obediently sat and looked straight into the camera as Emily began to click away.

"I've finished the film now — I'll ask Dad if he'll drop it off in Compton on Monday morning." Emily patted Pirate, who was still sitting patiently in his basket. "We should be able to pick up the photos after school."

"Good boy, Pirate!" Neil fished in his pocket for a couple of treats to reward the dog for behaving so well. To his surprise, as soon as Pirate spotted the treats he sat up on his back legs. Neil threw him one of the biscuits, and Pirate caught it easily. Then the mongrel slid down on his front paws so that his nose touched the ground, as if he was taking a bow in front of an audience. Neil and Emily could hardly believe their eyes.

"Isn't he smart?" Emily cried.

"His owner must have taught him to do tricks."

Neil threw another treat to Pirate, and once again
the dog caught it and took a bow.

"I wonder what else he can do?" Emily asked
eagerly.

Neil frowned. "Trouble is, we don't know the hand
or voice signals that he's been trained with."

"Try something else," Emily urged him.

Neil thought for a minute. "Pirate!" he called, getting the dog's attention. "Roll!"

Pirate immediately lay on the floor of the pen and
rolled over, showing his fat tummy. Then he rolled
back over in the opposite direction, jumped to his
feet, and looked up at Neil as if to say, *That was easy!*

"I bet he can do tons of tricks," Emily said as Neil rewarded Pirate with another dog treat. "It's such a shame we don't know them all."

"Well, we can try to find out —" Neil began, scratching his nose. Then he stopped, amazed. Pirate had spotted what Neil was doing and had started scratching *his* nose, too.

"That's awesome! We'll have to put this on the web site! Maybe then he'll find a new owner," Emily said hopefully. "Everyone loves a dog who can do tricks!"

Neil nodded. It was important that they made sure potential owners knew how amazing Pirate was. The dog's future depended on it.

"Sarah, will you *please* get out from under my feet!" Carole Parker said distractedly as she put a large baking pan of cake mixture into the oven. Neil grinned. Sarah was being even more annoying than usual this morning. Not only was she still going on about Disney World, she was also trying to persuade their mother not to give the large cake she was making to the Morrises.

"But chocolate cake is my *favorite!*" Sarah grumbled. "Why do you have to give it to those new people? Neil and Emily said they're horrible!"

"Dad, is it OK if I bring Jake to the obedience class this morning?" Neil asked, pouring himself some cornflakes. His father held regular obedience classes for dogs in Red's Barn on Wednesday nights and

Sunday mornings. Jake was already pretty well-trained in the basic commands, but Neil still liked to join in the classes occasionally.

"Sure," his father agreed as he sat down at the kitchen table. "And you might want to look in on Pirate this morning," he added. "He was barking last night. Probably misses his owner."

"Was he?" Neil was surprised. "I didn't hear him."

"Neither did I," Emily said. She was leafing through a book called *How to Teach Your Old Dog New Tricks.*

"Well, I think we're all too used to doggy noises to get woken up, unless it's really loud," Bob replied. "But Pirate could probably use a bit of company."

"He's really smart, Dad," Emily said eagerly. "Someone taught him to do a lot of tricks."

Bob laughed. "Really?"

"Dad, what's going to happen to the dogs when we go to Disney World?" Sarah asked innocently, going over to put an arm around her father's neck.

Bob shook his head at her. "Sarah, dear, we haven't decided *where* we're going on vacation yet."

"If we did go to America, though, we could visit the Hammonds and Delilah," Emily put in, seizing her chance. "*And* Max and Prince."

Carole rolled her eyes and put her hands on her hips. "Emily Parker, don't you start! Sarah's bad enough!"

"Oh, Mom —" Emily began, prepared to argue her case, but just then the doorbell rang.

Neil frowned. "Who's that? It's kind of early for visitors."

"I'll get it." His father got up from the table, but Neil also jumped up and followed him down the hall. It might be some crisis involving a dog, and if it was, Neil wanted to know all about it. He got a shock when Bob opened the front door to find Jo Morris standing there.

"Mr. Parker?" Jo asked frostily. She looked pale and tense and very uncomfortable. Neil glared at

her, wondering what in the world she was doing there. "I'm Jo Morris from Old Mill Farm."

"Pleased to meet you," Bob Parker said pleasantly, and extended a friendly hand. After a moment's hesitation, Jo Morris shook it. But Neil could tell from the set of his father's shoulders that he was expecting trouble. "Come in."

"I won't, thank you." Jo Morris folded her arms. "This isn't a social visit. It's about your dogs, Mr. Parker. They kept me and my family awake half the night with their barking."

Neil clenched his fists. *What a bunch of baloney,* he thought angrily. It had only been Pirate that was barking, and it couldn't have been that loud if it hadn't woken *him* up. Jo Morris was obviously exaggerating.

"Well, I don't think the noise was that bad," Bob said in a steely but polite voice. "We've just taken in a dog whose owner has died and he did bark last night, but I'm sure he'll settle down soon."

Jo Morris blushed and looked even more uncomfortable. "Well, I'm sorry to hear that, but I'm afraid it's not good enough, Mr. Parker." Her blush deepened. "We moved out here for the peace and quiet, not to listen to dogs barking all night. And while we're on the subject of dogs, we don't want you walking any of your animals on Old Mill Farm land from now on, public footpath or no public footpath. Do I make myself clear?"

## CHAPTER THREE

**N**eil was so angry he couldn't control himself. How *dare* Jo Morris march into King Street Kennels and tell them that they couldn't walk their dogs on a public footpath!

"You can't do that!" he snapped.

"Neil," his father said calmly, but there was a warning in his tone and Neil kept quiet, even though he was seething inside. Who did Jo Morris think she was? She'd only been at Old Mill Farm for five minutes and already she was throwing her weight around.

"Is everything OK?" Carole came to the door to find out what was going on, with a curious Emily and Sarah following behind her.

"No, it isn't," Bob Parker said levelly. He didn't raise his voice, but Neil could tell that his dad was

**27**

very angry indeed. "I don't want to argue about this, Mrs. Morris. After all, we're neighbors. But it *is* a public footpath, and you'll find it very difficult to stop everyone in Compton from walking their dogs on your land."

Jo Morris looked a little embarrassed. "Yes, I realize that," she blustered. "But in the meantime, I'd be very grateful if you could exercise your dogs somewhere else — or I may have to take alternative action."

Then she spun around on her heel and marched off up the Parkers' driveway.

"Dad! She can't keep us off the footpath, can she?" Neil asked anxiously as his father closed the door.

"No, she can't," Bob Parker said firmly. "That's what a public footpath is — for the public!"

Carole was grim-faced. "She just about stopped short of threatening us with legal action," she said. "How dare she?"

"She was like that when Neil and I met her yesterday," Emily added.

"She *is* horrible!" Sarah said, her eyes wide.

"What are we going to do, Dad?" Neil asked.

"We'll keep away from the footpath again today, and let Jo Morris calm down a bit," his father replied. "She's the one who's in the wrong, and when she's calmed down she might be a bit more reasonable."

Neil didn't think so. *And why should we keep away from the footpath when we have a perfect right to be there?* he thought furiously.

"And in the meantime," Carole said, heading for the kitchen, "we'll eat that chocolate cake ourselves!"

"Yay!" Sarah shouted, delighted, and ran after her mother.

Neil frowned. He had a bad feeling that Jo Morris meant trouble for King Street Kennels. Big trouble.

"Neil!" Emily was hanging out of the living room window, waving an envelope at him. "Jake's registration papers from the Kennel Club are here!"

"Oh, excellent!" Neil broke into a run, Jake and Pirate bounding along beside him. It was Monday morning, and Neil had gotten up early to take the two dogs for a walk in the park before school.

"The mailman was just here," Emily said breathlessly as Neil hurtled in through the front door, the dogs at his heels. "Quick, open it!"

"Give me a chance!" Neil grinned. He'd had no problems registering Jake as a pedigree dog with the Kennel Club because, when he'd managed to trace Sam's original owner, he'd discovered that his beloved dog had a champion pedigree. It was lucky, too, that the papers had come just in time for Jake to be entered in the upcoming agility competition.

"What name did they give you?" Emily asked, jumping up and down impatiently. Neil had had to choose three possible names under which to register Jake, in case one of them had been used before by someone else.

Neil tore open the envelope and pulled out the slip of paper inside. "Samsboy Puppy Patrol Jake," he read out. "That was my first choice!"

"Did you hear that, Jake?" Emily kneeled down and put her arm around Jake's furry neck. "That's your official, registered name!"

Pirate gave a bark, cocked his head to one side, and looked up at Neil as if to say, *Don't I get an official name, too?* Neil laughed and scratched Pirate's floppy ears.

"I don't think you could pass for a pedigree dog, Pirate," he said, "But you're the best, all the same."

It was a scramble for Neil to eat his breakfast and get ready for school after all the excitement. He managed to swallow a few bites of toast, then he jumped onto his bike and pedaled like the wind down the road that led into Compton. As usual, he was meeting his best friend Chris Wilson on the way.

"Hi, Neil." Chris was waiting for him, and looked amused to see his friend red in the face and panting hard. "What's up, buddy? You look like you've just biked all the way from London to Compton!"

"I didn't want to be late," Neil wheezed.

"Good weekend?" Chris asked as they biked off together.

Neil made a face. "Not exactly . . ."

As they made their way into Compton, Neil told Chris about Jo Morris and everything that had happened over the weekend. Chris was almost as indignant as Neil.

"They can't just stop people from using the footpath!" he exclaimed. "They've got no right!"

"I know," Neil said grimly as he and Chris cycled up Jarvis Road toward the school. "Dad's going to call Sergeant Moorhead and ask him about it." Sergeant Moorhead was the head of the Compton police department and knew the Parkers very well. "I just hope he can work it out —" Neil stopped speaking suddenly and gave a groan.

"What's up?" asked Chris.

"That's her," Neil muttered. "Jo Morris!"

Mrs. Morris was standing outside the school gates, along with a nervous-looking Tom and Vicky, who were both wearing Meadowbank School uniforms. Neil had forgotten that the Morris children would probably join their school — he just hoped that Vicky wasn't in his class.

As Neil and Chris climbed off their bikes and wheeled them toward the gates, Neil noticed that Jo was chatting to Julie Baker's mom. Julie was Emily's best friend. Neil was really curious to hear what they were saying, and he couldn't help edging a bit closer to find out.

"So, how are you settling in?" Mrs. Baker was asking.

"Well, all right, I suppose," Jo Morris replied. "But there's such a lot to do. The house was completely gutted by the fire, so we're virtually rebuilding it. And, of course, living next door to that awful kennel doesn't help."

Neil tensed and glanced over at Chris, who raised his eyebrows.

"What, King Street, you mean?" Mrs. Baker sounded surprised. "Haven't you met the Parkers yet? They're a very nice family."

"Well . . . er . . . yes," Jo Morris muttered. "But I just don't like having all those dogs nearby. I'm sure it's not very hygienic, and they keep us awake with their barking."

"King Street Kennels is very clean," Mrs. Baker

said firmly. "And I know the dogs are very well taken care of. Maybe you should go and see for yourself."

Jo Morris blushed, and she turned even redder when she spotted Neil glaring at her. "Come on, you two," she said quickly, turning to Vicky and Tom. "It's time we went into school and met your new teachers."

Vicky and Tom were pink with embarrassment themselves as they glanced from Neil to their mother. Vicky smiled timidly at Neil as if to apologize for her mother's rude remarks. Neil felt a bit sorry for her, but he couldn't bring himself to smile back. He was seething. How *dare* Jo Morris bad-mouth King Street Kennels! But at least Mrs. Baker had stuck up for them. Jo Morris would find out just how popular King Street Kennels were in Compton if she went around making comments like that.

Chris gave a low whistle. "I see what you mean!" he said. "Boy, Jo Morris really does have it in for King Street, doesn't she?"

Neil nodded. He was still speechless with anger.

"What nerve! I'm glad Tom Morris isn't in my class," Emily said indignantly. It was late afternoon, and they were out in the exercise field with Jake. Neil had set up the obstacle course as soon as he'd gotten home from school, and he and Jake had been practicing for the last hour or so. Emily had come to join them, and Neil had told her about what had happened that morning.

"Well, it's not exactly Tom and Vicky's fault," Neil pointed out reasonably. "But I'm pretty glad Vicky isn't in my class, either, or I might have told her exactly what I think of her mom!"

"Jo Morris shouldn't be allowed to go around talking about King Street Kennels like that!" Emily said angrily. "How can we stop her, Neil?"

Neil shrugged. "We can't."

"Dad called Sergeant Moorhead," Emily went on, "and he said that as long as our dogs are on leashes and are well-behaved, he didn't think there was anything Jo Morris could do."

"That won't stop her complaining, though," Neil muttered.

"Well, I don't think we should let her boss us around!" Emily's eyes met Neil's. "I think we should take Jake for his walk now, don't you?"

Neil looked hard at his sister. "You mean . . . ?"

Emily squared her shoulders. "Yes, I do! I think we should take Jake along the *public* footpath!"

Neil grinned at her. "You know what Dad said."

Emily looked at him challengingly. "Dad said to keep away from it *yesterday*. He didn't say anything about *today*. So are you coming or not?"

"Try and stop me!" Neil replied, and whistled to Jake so that he could attach the collie's leash. They walked across the field toward the gate, and Emily swung it open.

"Here goes!" she said as they stepped onto Old Mill Farm land.

Neil's stomach was churning as they set off along the footpath. It wasn't that he was scared of Jo Morris, but he knew how she'd react if she saw them. This time, Neil told himself, they'd be ready for her.

"Look, the builders are just leaving," Emily whispered to Neil as they approached the house. The builders were packing up for the day, having erected scaffolding all around the fire-damaged building, but there was no sign of the Morris family.

Just then, however, the door of the trailer flew open with a loud crash, making Neil, Emily, and even Jake jump. A red-faced Jo Morris rushed out, followed by her husband, Vicky, and Tom.

"What are you doing here?" Jo asked tightly, glaring at Neil and Emily. She was obviously struggling to keep her temper. "I thought I told you not to walk your dogs on our land!"

"Hang on, Jo," Graham Morris said under his breath. "Vicky, Tom, go back inside the trailer and shut the door."

"But, Dad —" Vicky began.

"Inside, now!" Graham snapped, and Vicky and Tom reluctantly did as they were told.

"This is a public footpath and we're the public, so we're allowed to use it," Emily said boldly.

"Sergeant Moorhead said you can't stop us!" Neil added.

Jo looked uncomfortable when Neil mentioned the policeman's name. "And what else did Sergeant Moorhead say?" she muttered.

"He said that if we keep our dogs under control and they're not a nuisance, there's nothing you can do!" Neil replied.

"Oh, really!" Jo Morris suddenly looked triumphant. "Well, what's Sergeant Moorhead going to say when he finds out that King Street Kennels have been letting their dogs loose to roam all over Old Mill Farm land?"

# CHAPTER FOUR

**N**eil and Emily stared at Jo Morris. They had no clue what she was talking about.

"What do you mean?" Neil asked. "We *never* let our dogs out on their own!"

Jo Morris raised her eyebrows. "Well, why have we seen a puppy running around loose for the last day or two?" she demanded. "It *must* be from King Street Kennels, and I think it's absolutely disgraceful —"

"Jo, calm down dear," her husband muttered.

"You don't know if the puppy's from King Street," Emily broke in angrily. "It could be a stray."

"And anyway, we don't have any puppies in the kennel or the rescue center at the moment," Neil added, his mind quickly running through all the dogs who were currently in the Parkers' care. He stared defiantly at Jo. "So it *can't* be one of ours!"

Jo didn't look convinced at all. "Well, I think it's *very* suspicious that we're living right next door to some kennel, and there's a stray dog on the loose," she said coldly. "I'm sure the police and the ASPCA would be interested to know that King Street Kennels don't look after their dogs properly." And on that threatening note, she stormed off.

Neil was so angry he could hardly speak. "We *do* look after our dogs properly, and it isn't one of ours!" He glared at Jo Morris's back. "Come on, Em, let's get out of here."

Emily nodded and walked off. Neil was about to follow her when Graham Morris hurried over to him, looking sheepish.

"Look, you two, it really would be better if you walked your dogs somewhere else from now on," he muttered as Jake snuffled around his sneakers in a friendly way. "It would save a lot of hassle."

"Not for us," Neil replied. "That's why the footpath's here. So we can use it as a shortcut across the fields."

Graham Morris sighed. "All this is getting totally out of hand."

Neil wanted to say, *And whose fault is that?* But he knew it would sound rude, so he bit his lip and kept quiet. As he turned to go, though, Neil saw something very interesting out of the corner of his eye. Graham Morris bent down to give Jake a quick pat.

Neil was shocked. He'd thought that Graham hated dogs as much as Jo did, but here he was being friendly to Jake. Graham Morris looked very embarrassed when he realized that Neil had spotted him. He straightened up quickly and hurried off into the trailer as fast as he could.

"What nerve!" Emily was ranting as Neil and Jake caught up with her.

"Yeah, well, I don't think Graham Morris is as anti-dogs as Jo is," Neil replied, and he told Emily what he'd just seen.

"Do you think Jo Morris is making it up? About

the puppy, I mean?" Emily asked Neil as they walked back toward the exercise field.

"I don't know." Neil was worried. If Jo Morris *was* making it up to try to damage the good name of King Street Kennels, she could do a lot of harm. But if she wasn't, it meant that there was a stray puppy running around who might be in danger. Neither situation was a good one.

Back at King Street Kennels, Neil and Emily found their mom and dad having a cup of tea in the kitchen with Kate Paget, the other kennel assistant. Carole took one look at Neil and Emily, and raised an eyebrow. "Don't tell me! You've been on the Old Mill Farm footpath again!"

"Well, Dad didn't say we had to keep off it *forever*," Emily said defensively.

"Bob and Carole have just been telling me all about it," Kate said, looking concerned. "Has Mrs. Morris calmed down yet?"

"Not exactly," Neil replied, and he told them about the new accusations Jo had made and the stray puppy she said she'd seen. As he spoke, he could see his parents' faces getting angrier and angrier.

"The nerve of that woman!" Carole burst out when Neil had finished. "How dare she assume that the dog was from King Street!"

"She's certainly got it in for us." Bob sighed. "We're going to have to be extra-careful from now on, and do everything by the book. If she complains to the Town Council, she could get us into trouble."

"I don't think Graham Morris feels the same way, though," Neil added, and he described the way Jo's husband had pet Jake. The Border collie, who was lying under the table, wagged his tail eagerly at the sound of his name.

"Perhaps that's the best way to try and work this out, then," Bob said grimly. "If Graham Morris is a bit more reasonable than his wife, we might have a chance of talking this through."

"But Dad, do you think Jo really saw a stray puppy on her land?" Neil asked anxiously. "Or do you think she was making it up?"

Kate looked thoughtful. "It's funny you should say that, Neil," she remarked, flicking her long blond hair out of her eyes, "because Glen thought he heard a puppy whimpering when he took Willow for a walk up on the hill last night." Glen was Kate's husband, and Willow was their little white dog.

Neil sat up in his chair. "What happened?"

"Well, it was starting to get dark, so Glen couldn't see very much when he looked," Kate explained. "But he said it definitely sounded like a puppy, and he was surprised because there weren't any people around."

Neil looked worried. He hated the thought of a puppy trying to cope on its own out in the countryside. It would be touch and go whether it could survive for very long.

"Dad, what are we going to do?" Emily asked, looking as concerned as Neil.

"I'll call the ASPCA." Bob got up from his chair. "Terri McCall, the officer there, will know if a puppy's been reported missing, or she might have heard about any other sightings. I'll call Mike Turner, too."

"OK, Dad," Neil said gratefully, all thoughts of Jo Morris immediately banished from his mind. He was far more anxious about the puppy at the moment.

"Come on, Neil." Emily slid out of her seat, too. "Let's go and scan Pirate's photo onto the web site. We can also write some stuff about the tricks he can do."

Neil followed his sister into the office. He switched on the computer, hoping desperately that Terri or Mike would be able to give them some leads about the puppy.

"Check the e-mails first," Emily suggested as she leafed through the photos of Pirate, searching for the best one. "I haven't looked at them for days."

While Neil was waiting for their e-mails to download, Bob stuck his head in the door.

"Did you find out anything, Dad?" Neil asked eagerly.

His father nodded. "Yes, I did. No one's reported a missing puppy, but Terri says several people have called her to say they've seen a small black-and-white dog wandering around the countryside."

Neil's heart lurched. "Did they say where?"

"In the vicinity of the park, the Old Mill Farm footpath, and King Street Kennels," Bob replied. "So it looks as if Jo Morris wasn't making it up after all."

*The stray puppy just has to be found as soon as possible*, Neil thought anxiously as his father went out. He would keep a sharp lookout when he took the dogs for walks, and he'd go out on his bike to search the surrounding area, too.

Still worrying about the puppy, Neil glanced absently through the King Street Kennels e-mails. None of them looked very interesting at first. . . . But suddenly, his eyes widened.

"Hey, Em!" he gasped. "Come and look at this!"

Curious, Emily came to read the long e-mail over Neil's shoulder. Her eyes lit up as she scanned it. "Wow, that's amazing!" she said. "Quick, Neil, print it out! We've got to show Mom and Dad!"

"All right, all right!" Neil grinned, switching on the printer. As soon as the sheets of paper came through, Neil grabbed them and they both ran into the kitchen. Kate had left, and Bob and Carole were having another cup of tea while Sarah tried once again to persuade them that a trip to Disney World was a great idea.

"Mom!" Emily said excitedly. "Look at this e-mail!"

Neil thrust the papers into Carole's hand. "It's from some relatives of ours, the Simpsons. They live in Alaska and they run a husky dog retirement center and they've invited us to come and visit!"

Bob and Carole looked completely blank.

"What are you talking about, Neil?" Bob asked.

"We don't have any relatives called the Simpsons," Carole said suspiciously. "It must be a hoax."

"Just look at the e-mail, Mom," Emily said impatiently. "They've put a family tree at the bottom so you can work out who they are."

Still looking bewildered, Carole stared at the papers. Then her face lit up. "I don't believe it! They're related to your great-grandmother's second cousin, Annabel Reid. I never did know what happened to that branch of the family."

"Where's Alaska?" Sarah asked curiously.

"In America, Squirt," Neil said.

"America!" Sarah's face lit up. "Is it near Disney World?"

Bob was looking interested now. "Read it out loud, Carole."

Carole cleared her throat.

*"Hi there, Parker family!*

*We came across your King Street Kennels web site by accident, but we think we might be related to you, as the family tree at the bottom of this page will show.*

*My name's Russell Simpson, and my wife Kim and*

*I run a husky dog retirement center here in Alaska
with our twelve-year-old daughter Fran. We'd sure
love to meet up with you some time and show you our
beautiful husky dogs. So if you're ever thinking of visiting the States, you must come and stay with us.
Kind of weird, isn't it, that both of our families work
with dogs?*

*We'll be looking out for your e-mail!*

*Best regards,*

*Russell, Kim, and Fran Simpson."*

"Mom!" Neil said excitedly as soon as Carole had
finished reading. "If we *did* go to America this summer, we could go and see the Simpsons in Alaska,
too." This trip to the United States was becoming
more interesting by the minute. Neil had never met
a real, live husky dog before.

"And don't forget Disney World!" Sarah added.

"Wait a minute!" Bob held up his hands. "We haven't
made any decisions yet, and anyway, there's no way
we could travel to all those different places during
one vacation. America's a huge country."

Sarah thought about that for a moment. "Well, I
don't mind going to Alaska instead of Disney World,"
she said hopefully. "I'd *love* to see the husky dogs."

"What do *you* think, Mom?" Emily asked eagerly.
"Are you going to reply to the Simpsons' e-mail?"

"Yes, of course I am," Carole said, still staring at
the message as if she couldn't quite believe it. "How

amazing that they came across the King Street Kennels web site by accident!"

Neil nudged Emily and grinned at her. Their mother looked really excited at discovering their long-lost relatives. "Maybe there's a chance we'll make it to America after all!" he whispered in his sister's ear. A trip to the U.S. would be something really exciting to look forward to.

# CHAPTER FIVE

**"W**hat's Jo Morris doing *now*?" Neil muttered to Chris as they came out of school and crossed the playground.

It was Thursday, three days after Neil and Emily had first heard about the missing puppy, and relations between the Parkers and the Morris family hadn't improved at all. Jo had been on the phone every day complaining about dog mess and noise, and about the stray puppy who had been seen on Old Mill Farm again. Neil was fed up with it all. He didn't want anything to do with the Morris family from now on. All he wanted was to find the puppy and make sure it was all right. He had been out every evening after school with Emily and Chris, searching the park, but they hadn't seen a thing.

Chris squinted across the playground. "Looks like she's giving everyone bits of paper," he said, puzzled.

Jo Morris was standing by the school gate, handing out what looked like printed letters to all the parents who'd come to meet their children. Neil wondered what was going on.

"Maybe she's trying to find out if anyone knows anything about the stray puppy," Chris suggested.

"Yeah, maybe. . . ." But Neil wasn't convinced. Why would Jo Morris worry about a stray puppy and go to all the trouble of printing leaflets about it? She didn't even *like* dogs. "Come on, let's go and take a look."

Vicky and Tom Morris were standing by the gate with their mom. Neil could see that they weren't too happy. Vicky was hopping impatiently from foot to foot as if she wished she was somewhere a million miles away, while Tom was kicking the bottom of the gate gloomily. When they saw Neil and Chris walking toward them, both of them turned bright red with embarrassment and started whispering to each other. Neil began to feel really worried. What was Jo Morris up to?

He soon found out.

"Hey, Neil!" Hasheem Lindon, one of Neil's classmates, rushed up to him, waving one of the papers in the air. "Have you seen what they're saying about King Street Kennels?"

His heart sinking, Neil grabbed the paper and read it.

### KING STREET KENNELS

*Are you as concerned as we are about stray dogs, dog mess, noise, and lack of hygiene? We believe King Street Kennels is guilty of all these things and that it's time they were stopped. We are starting a petition requesting that action be taken against the kennel by the Town Council. If you are interested in joining our campaign, please contact Jo Morris at Old Mill Farm.*

Neil could hardly believe his eyes.

"This is all a pack of lies!" he said in a voice that trembled with rage.

"Cool it, Neil," Hasheem said reassuringly. "Everyone knows that Puppy Patrol is the best! No one will pay any attention to this."

But Neil was too furious to listen. Scrunching the paper into a ball, he ran over to Jo Morris, who was still handing out leaflets to groups of rather bemused-looking parents.

"What are you *doing*?" he snapped.

Jo Morris turned around quickly and glared at him. "This has nothing to do with you, Neil."

"Of course it does!" Neil yelled, not even trying to

keep calm. "You're telling a whole lot of lies about King Street Kennels!"

"They're not lies —" Jo began, just as Emily rushed over to them, white-faced.

"Neil, have you seen this?" she cried waving a leaflet.

"Yes, I have," Neil said grimly. He stared furiously at Jo. "And you're not going to get away with it!"

Jo opened her mouth to reply, but then she realized that everyone was silently watching what was going on. She turned to Vicky and Tom, quickly

bundling the rest of the leaflets into her bag. "Come on, you two."

Vicky and Tom looked miserable as they followed their mom to the car. They were both way too uncomfortable even to look at Neil and Emily. Neil watched them drive off, his heart pounding with anger. There had to be laws to stop people like Jo Morris from going around saying things that just weren't true.

"Who does this woman think she is?" Carole Parker tore the leaflet neatly into eight pieces and tossed it into the kitchen trash can. "That's where that belongs — with the rest of the garbage!"

Sarah and Emily cheered, and even Neil couldn't help smiling. "I think most of the parents and kids outside the school threw theirs away, too, Mom," he said, his hand on Jake's head. The Border collie always seemed to sense when Neil was upset, and he was sitting close to his owner, his warm body pressed against Neil's legs.

Carole glanced at her husband. "What are we going to do about this, Bob?"

"I'll have to speak to Andrew," Neil's father said soberly. Andrew Stewart was the Parkers' lawyer.

Carole groaned. "Well, that means a hefty bill, for sure! Maybe just a warning letter from Andrew to Jo will do the trick, and she'll stop this ridiculous campaign."

"I'll give him a call now," said Bob, going out of the room.

"Did you e-mail the Simpsons, Mom?" Emily asked.

"Yes, I did, actually," her mother replied. "Several times this week. We've been catching up on family news. I have to say, they seem very nice."

"So are we going to Alaska or not?" Sarah asked impatiently.

"Oh, come on, Mom!" said Emily.

Carole shook her head. "Give it a rest, you guys," she said, but she was smiling.

Emily nudged Neil. "I bet we've got a good chance," she whispered.

"Yeah." Neil wasn't sure how he felt. Did he really want to leave King Street Kennels while all this stuff with Jo Morris was going on? How would their Uncle Jack, who ran the kennel when the Parkers were away, cope with Jo and her campaign?

After they'd eaten, Neil decided it was time for a training session for Jake, and for Pirate, too. He'd been so busy looking for the stray puppy over the last few days that he hadn't spent much time with Pirate. He thought it might be interesting to see if the little dog had been taught any agility skills along with the tricks he'd learned.

Emily went to the exercise field with him and helped him set up the obstacle course. Jake was already getting excited, jumping around their legs and swishing his tail back and forth. He always looked forward to his training sessions.

"Should we go and look for the stray puppy again after the training session?" Emily asked as she stood the tire upright and fixed it in place with some bricks.

Neil nodded. "Good idea. Go and get Pirate, will you, Em? I'll finish setting up the course."

Emily nodded, and Neil finished building the see-saw. Then he whistled to Jake, who was sniffing around in the hedge-bushes.

"OK, Jake, let's see how much you remember."

As Jake bounded over to him, Neil happened to glance across at Old Mill Farm. Then he frowned. He thought he'd seen something moving through the long grass near the footpath. Yes! There it was again!

Hardly daring to breathe, Neil kept his eyes fixed on the spot. Then, all of a sudden, a very small black-and-white dog jumped out of the middle of the clump of grass and trotted off in the direction of Old Mill Farm.

"The stray puppy!" Neil breathed, his heart beginning to thump. "It must be!"

He raced across the field to the gate. Jake was right behind him, and Neil kneeled down and quickly fastened the leash to his collar. He knew he was wasting precious seconds, but he couldn't risk Jake

running loose on Old Mill Farm land. Jo Morris would go nuts if she saw them.

"Neil!" Emily was running across the field toward him with Pirate. "What's going on?"

"The puppy!" Neil straightened up and looked over the gate. To his utter frustration, the pup was nowhere to be seen. "It was over there in that long grass!"

"Quick!" Emily yanked open the gate. "He must still be around somewhere."

They searched the area around the long clumps of grass, but the puppy seemed to have vanished into thin air. Neil bit his lip in annoyance. If only he hadn't stopped to put on Jake's leash. . . .

"Do you think the puppy went toward the farm-house?" Emily asked.

"I hope not," Neil replied, "because Jo Morris won't be too pleased! Let's look along the footpath."

For the next hour, Neil and Emily walked along the path, searching carefully under bushes and behind trees. Pirate and Jake thought it was all a great game.

"This is hopeless," Neil muttered as they finally gave up and headed back toward the exercise field. "How could a puppy vanish just like that?"

Emily nudged him. "Look," she whispered.

Vicky and Tom Morris were standing near the gate that led into the exercise field.

"Hello," Vicky called timidly as Neil and Emily got closer. Emily muttered a reluctant hello, but Neil didn't say anything. He hadn't forgotten about Jo Morris's leaflets.

"Hey, he's a funny dog!" Tom said, staring at Pirate.

"No, he's not," Neil snapped.

Tom looked taken aback. "Can I pet him?" he asked quickly, as if he was trying to make amends.

Neil shrugged, which Tom took as a yes. He patted Pirate's head, and the dog licked his fingers in a friendly way.

"You're so lucky having so many dogs," Tom said enviously as Pirate presented his plump tummy to be tickled. "I wish I lived at a kennel."

"Well, it's hard work," Neil replied, thawing a little. After all, it wasn't Vicky and Tom's fault that their mom was a pain in the neck. "But we like it."

Jake was pawing Tom's leg, demanding some attention, too, and Neil couldn't help smiling when Tom put an arm around both dogs and let them lick his face enthusiastically. Jo Morris would have a fit if she could see him now!

"We saw you looking around," Vicky said as she bent down to give Pirate a pat. She was obviously trying to be friendly, but she seemed oddly jumpy at the same time and kept glancing over her shoulder at the farmhouse. "Have you lost something?"

"Neil saw the stray puppy," Emily replied. "But he got away."

Vicky and Tom both looked worried, and Neil began to like them even more. If they were concerned about the pup, then they couldn't be that bad.

"Have *you* seen the puppy?" Emily asked.

Vicky blinked. "No, we haven't seen him, have we, Tom?"

"No," Tom muttered, burying his face in Jake's shaggy neck.

Neil frowned. Vicky and Tom *seemed* to want to be friendly, but they were behaving a bit strangely. Maybe, he thought wryly, they were worried their mom might catch them talking to the enemy from King Street.

"How many dogs do you have in the kennel right now?" Tom asked.

"Why don't you come and have a look?" Neil said, surprising himself with his own invitation. But at least then Vicky and Tom would see how well-run the kennel was. "You could come back with us now."

"Oh!" Vicky and Tom looked at each other.

"We'd like to," Vicky began.

"But we can't," Tom went on.

"We're going shopping with our dad," Vicky added quickly, just as Tom said, "We've got to go and do our homework."

Neil stared at them, and Vicky and Tom looked sheepish.

"You don't *have* to come," Neil said coldly. "It was just an idea."

"No, we want to," Vicky stammered. "We just can't come *now*."

"What about this time tomorrow?" Tom asked.

Neil shrugged. "OK."

"See you then," Vicky said, and they ran off toward the farmhouse.

"Weird!" Neil said, shaking his head. "What's wrong with *them*?"

"They were probably scared their mom would catch them talking to us," Emily replied as she led the dogs into the exercise field. "They must know she wouldn't like them visiting the kennel."

"Yeah, I guess you're right." Neil glanced across

the field just in time to see Vicky and her brother disappear behind the water-mill. He did feel sorry for the two of them — they obviously liked dogs, even if their mother didn't. But right now, he was much more concerned about the stray puppy. . . .

**CHAPTER SIX**

"**M**om, has anyone phoned or e-mailed about Pirate?" Neil asked as soon as he came in from school the following afternoon. It had been a few days now since they'd put Pirate's photo up on the kennel's web site, along with details of the tricks he could perform.

"I'm afraid not, Neil," Carole replied.

Neil bit his lip. He'd taken Pirate through the obstacle course with Jake yesterday evening and, although he'd never done it before, the funny little dog had been quick to learn and surprisingly sure-footed. *Pirate has so much going for him*, Neil thought. He just knew any owner would love the dog if only they could see past his slightly unusual looks.

59

Neil glanced at his mom, who was banging pots and pans around the kitchen, looking stressed out.

Emily was sitting at the table. "Dad went over to see Jo Morris," she said in a low voice. "She called today, complaining *again*."

"Well, I just hope the mention of lawyers makes her see things more clearly," Carole muttered.

Neil hoped so, too. "Come on, Jake." He stood up, and the Border collie glanced up at him, his dark eyes alert. "Let's go over to the exercise field. The obstacle course is still set up from yesterday."

"I'll come with you," Emily volunteered. "I'm really worried about the puppy," she went on as they left the house. "If only we'd caught him!"

"I know." Neil felt depressed. "He's been living in the wild for at least a week. How much longer can he survive?"

"I don't even want to think about it." Emily shuddered.

Neil was glad to see that all their problems didn't seem to be affecting Jake. The Border collie's tail was wagging like crazy as he waited patiently for Neil's signal at the start of the course.

"Go, Jake, go!" Neil shouted, and immediately Jake shot across the homemade bridge. He soared over the jumps and through the tire. Neil ran around with him, making sure Jake stopped and sat whenever he was supposed to. There would be certain places on the course, called contact points, where the dogs had to stay still. If they didn't manage to stay for a certain length of time, they would pick up penalty points.

"Good job, Jake!" Neil yelled proudly as the collie sailed easily over the last hurdle. "Bravo, boy!"

Jake immediately rushed over to his owner to be pet, looking incredibly pleased with himself. Neil grinned, and ruffled the thick fur around the young dog's neck. There were still some things that needed work, but, on the whole, Jake was proving to be a real champ.

"You're going to do great in the competition, Jake!" he murmured as the collie pushed his wet nose lovingly into Neil's hand.

A burst of applause from the other side of the field made Neil look around in surprise. Vicky and Tom Morris were perched on the gate, watching everything that was going on.

"That was awesome!" Vicky called. "Your dog's super smart, Neil!"

"Thanks." Neil couldn't help smiling.

"Is it hard to teach dogs to do those kinds of tricks?" Tom wanted to know.

"It can be," Neil admitted as Vicky and her brother slid off the gate and came to join them. "But Border collies are very intelligent, so that makes it easier."

"Um . . . did you know your dad came to see our parents?" Vicky asked in an apologetic tone.

Neil nodded, not trusting himself to speak.

"Your mom's really got it in for King Street Kennels," Emily pointed out bluntly. "Do you know why she hates dogs so much?"

Tom shook his head miserably, then glanced at his sister.

"Mom's in a really bad mood these days," Vicky mumbled. "The builders are getting on her nerves, and the trailer's too cramped."

Neil thought those were pretty lame excuses for starting a campaign against King Street Kennels, but he didn't say so. "Do you want to come over and visit the kennel now?" he offered.

Once again, Vicky and Tom looked nervous.

"We can't," Vicky said at last. "We've got something else to do."

"Is it because your mom wouldn't like it?" Emily asked sympathetically.

"Yes, that's it," Vicky agreed quickly. "Mom told us to keep away from the kennel."

"Well, you're in our exercise field," Neil pointed out. There was definitely something funny going on here, but he couldn't figure out what.

Meanwhile, Jake was sniffing around Tom's legs, his tail wagging as if he could smell something exciting. Then Neil saw the Border collie stick his muzzle into the pocket of Tom's trousers and pull out an open bag of dog treats.

"Jake! Drop!" Neil said sternly.

"Oh!" Tom turned pale as Jake obediently dropped

the treats on the grass. He grabbed them and stuffed them back into his pocket, flashing a guilty look at Vicky as he did so. "Um . . . thanks."

Puzzled, Neil glanced at Emily. Why in the world would Tom have a bag of dog treats in his pocket?

"Tom . . ." Vicky said, nodding frantically at her brother, "you bought those for Jake, didn't you?"

Tom looked blank, then his face cleared. "Oh, yes, I did." He quickly fished the bag out of his pocket again, and gave Jake a couple of the treats. Neil watched in silence. He didn't believe a word of it. If the dog treats were for Jake, why was the bag already open? It didn't make sense.

"We've got to go." Vicky grabbed her brother's arm and started pulling him away.

"That's weird," Emily remarked as Vicky and Tom climbed quickly over the gate again. "Did you believe any of that?"

"Nope." Neil watched Vicky and Tom skirt around the trailer and head toward the water mill. They disappeared around the side of it again, like they had done yesterday. "There's something funny going on, Em."

"Like what?"

Neil shrugged. He had his suspicions, but they seemed too absurd for words. "Maybe we should walk over to Old Mill Farm to meet Dad," he suggested pointedly.

Emily caught on immediately. "OK!" she said.

Neil's heart began to thump as they walked toward the water mill. They had to leave the public footpath to reach the house, and that meant they were trespassing, even though they had the excuse that they were meeting their dad. Bob wouldn't be very happy if he saw them, either. He was obviously still inside the trailer, discussing the situation with the Morrises. Neil hoped that no one would come out until they were safely back in the exercise field.

Emily hurried around the side of the farmhouse, and Neil followed with Jake. The builders were hard at work and didn't notice them at all. There was no sign of Vicky and Tom, but Neil noticed that Jake seemed very interested in a small, stone shed. He was straining at his leash, trying to pull Neil toward it.

Beckoning to Emily, Neil tiptoed over to the shed. The door was rickety and didn't close properly, and Neil could just about see through the narrow gap. What he saw made him catch his breath. Reaching for the handle, he pushed the door open.

Vicky and Tom Morris were sitting on some sacks on the floor, playing with a small black-and-white dog. Neil recognized it right away. It was the stray puppy he'd seen the day before.

Vicky and Tom glanced up as the door swung open, then gasped. When they saw Neil, Emily, and Jake standing there, they both looked very relieved.

"What are you doing here?" said Vicky. "We thought you were Mom!"

Tom was hugging the puppy tightly to his chest. "Quick, come in before someone sees you!" he hissed.

"Is that the stray puppy?" Emily asked, bewildered. Tom nodded.

"Keep hold of him, Tom," Neil said urgently. "I don't want him to go near Jake, in case he hasn't had his vaccinations."

Jake was looking very interested in the small bundle of fur in Tom's arms, but Neil looped the collie's leash over the door handle so that he was well away from the puppy.

"But what's he doing here?" Emily demanded, staring at the little dog.

"We found him yesterday afternoon," Vicky confessed. "It must have been just after you saw him, Neil."

"And we've been looking after him ever since," Tom added.

"I sort of guessed, because of the dog treats," Neil admitted. "But I didn't really think it could be true because . . ." He stopped.

"Because of our mom, you mean," Tom said flatly. "Because she hates dogs."

"Well, yeah," Neil agreed.

"Mom wouldn't hate Harry," Vicky said confidently, taking the puppy from Tom. He nestled down in the crook of her arm, gazing up at her trustingly with his large brown eyes. "No one could hate Harry!"

"Can I take a look at him?" Neil asked.

Vicky hesitated, then gave him the puppy. Gently, Neil checked him over. He looked like some sort of crossbreed terrier, and he was pretty young — only about sixteen weeks. The pup was way too thin, and his black-and-white fur was matted and dirty, but he had an appealing face, with big eyes and perky little ears. He lay quietly in Neil's arms, which was troubling. It was likely that the little dog was feeling weak and undernourished after his ordeal.

"So you call him Harry?" Emily said.

"Yes," Tom said proudly as Neil placed the puppy gently down on the floor. Harry immediately trotted over to a bowl of water and took a long drink. There was also a little saucer of dog food, as well as a cardboard box with a comfy cushion in the bottom for the puppy to sleep in.

"Harry should see a vet." Neil frowned. "And the sooner the better."

"But he's fine!" Vicky argued.

"Anyway, we can look after him," Tom added firmly.

"You can't keep him locked in the shed forever," Emily pointed out.

"We're going to ask Mom if we can keep him." Vicky looked defiantly at Neil.

Neil couldn't help giving a snort of disbelief. "You've got to be kidding!"

"She'll come around." Tom backed his sister up stoutly. "Dad likes dogs, and he'll love Harry."

Neil couldn't deny that, having seen Graham Morris be friendly to Jake. But Jo Morris? No way. He glanced at Emily, who shrugged. Neil knew what she was thinking. It wasn't worth arguing with Vicky and Tom. They were clearly so infatuated with Harry that they wouldn't face up to the fact that their mom wasn't going to let them keep him. Neil decided to try another approach.

"Harry must see a vet," he repeated firmly as

Emily kneeled down to pet the puppy. "He might have picked up an infection that isn't obvious yet. You don't want anything to happen to him, do you?"

Vicky and Tom looked alarmed and shook their heads.

"Well, how long are you planning to keep him here, then, before you tell your mom?" Neil went on. He knew he was being a bit aggressive, but the welfare of a dog was at stake.

"We thought we'd fatten him up a bit first," Vicky replied uncertainly.

"But you don't even know whether Harry's a stray or not," Emily pointed out as the puppy gave a huge yawn and toddled over to his bed. "His real owner might be looking for him."

"I never thought of that," Vicky said quietly while Tom stared miserably at the ground. Neil felt sorry for them, but he had to make sure that Harry was OK. Yes, the puppy was being looked after, but Neil would feel a lot happier if he could take him to Mike Turner right away.

"Sshh!" Emily said suddenly. "What's that?"

They all froze. Neil could hear the sound of raised voices, but he couldn't make out exactly what they were saying.

"It's Dad," he whispered. Bob and the Morrises must have come out of the trailer and, by the sound of it, they hadn't had a very friendly discussion.

"Quiet!" Vicky whispered, scooping Harry up.

Neil held his breath. He didn't like the idea of his dad and Jo Morris discovering them hiding in the shed with the stray puppy. Heart thumping, he glanced over at the door. Was it his imagination, or were the voices coming closer?

Then Neil's stomach gave a lurch. "Where's Jake?" he hissed frantically at Emily.

Emily's eyes widened as she looked over at the door, which was ajar. There was now no sign of the Border collie. "I thought you looped his leash over the door handle?"

"I did!" Neil groaned as he raced to the door. "He must have pulled it free."

Neil stood by the open door, breathing hard, and edged it open a bit wider. Where was Jake?

". . . And you can expect a letter from *my* lawyer, too, Mr. Parker," Neil heard Jo saying. He couldn't see anyone, but he assumed that his father and the Morrises were standing near the side of the farmhouse. "Then we'll see who's right and who's wrong!"

Neil's heart almost stopped beating as he spotted Jake nosing around the scaffolding at the back of the house. He didn't dare call out, but if he could just get Jake's attention, he could signal silently for the young dog to "come."

Before Neil had time to do that, something else happened. One of the builders was walking along

the narrow wooden platform that ran along the scaffolding. As he edged his way around, his foot caught a couple of stray bricks that were lying on the walkway. The bricks plummeted toward the ground, heading straight for Jake. . . .

# CHAPTER SEVEN

It was like a film in slow motion, Neil thought later. He saw the builder's boot connect with the bricks, he saw the bricks tip off the edge of the walkway, and he saw them fall straight toward Jake — who was too intent on sniffing around the scaffolding to notice.

*"Jake!"* Neil yelled urgently.

The Border collie looked up and bounded toward him just seconds before the bricks crashed to the ground. Jake jumped and cowered, whining, ears flat against his head. Relieved, Neil rushed over to him. He'd really given the game away now, but he'd had no choice. As he bent to comfort Jake, the others raced out of the shed and just barely managed to shut the door behind them before the Morrises and

Bob Parker appeared around the side of the farm-house.

"What's going on?" Jo Morris demanded. She stopped, hands on hips, and glared at Neil and Emily. "What are you two doing here?"

"I'd like to know that, too," Bob said tightly, his eyes burning into Neil's.

Neil's heart sank. His father was furious. "We just came to meet you, Dad," he muttered.

"But what are you doing *here*?" Jo said sarcasti-cally. "The back of our house isn't part of the public footpath!"

"They came to see us, Mom," Vicky volunteered bravely. "Neil and Emily are our friends."

"Oh." Jo looked a bit deflated.

"What was that crash?" Graham Morris asked.

"I knocked a couple of bricks off and nearly hit that dog there," the builder called from the scaffold-ing. "We *have* asked you to keep the kids away from the building work, Mr. Morris. . . ."

"I should have known that dog was to blame!" Jo Morris declared bitterly. "And Vicky, Tom, haven't we asked you to keep away from the back of the house? Come inside this minute!" She shepherded her children away, with Graham trailing dismally behind.

"It wasn't Jake's fault —" Emily began, but Neil nudged her in the ribs. They were by no means out of the woods with their dad yet.

"Sorry, Dad," Neil muttered, chasing after his father as Bob strode off toward the exercise field. "We just thought making friends with Tom and Vicky might help."

"I don't think anything's going to help at the moment, Neil," his dad said quietly. Neil could tell that Bob was making a big effort not to take his frustration with Jo Morris out on Neil and Emily. "So I'm telling you now — I don't want you going anywhere near Vicky and Tom and Old Mill Farm again for the time being. Do I make myself clear?"

Neil and Emily both nodded silently.

As they crossed the exercise field, Neil knew that some tough decisions were going to have to be made in the next few days about Harry. Jo Morris would never let Vicky and Tom keep the puppy, so they would have to hand Harry over to Terri at the ASPCA. If Vicky and Tom wouldn't agree, Neil would just have to call Terri himself. He wasn't looking forward to that.

"All right, Jake, let's call it a day." Neil sighed, and whistled to the Border collie. Jake trotted over to him, then jumped and whined as Neil accidentally knocked against the seesaw plank, sending it crashing to the ground.

Neil frowned. Jake was pretty jumpy at the moment, and had been ever since the brick incident yesterday. They'd come out this morning to practice the agility course again, but Neil could see that Jake's heart just wasn't in it. He made quite a few mistakes, and Neil thought it was better to forget about the course for the time being.

"Neil?" Emily hurried across the courtyard to meet them. "I've just put a description of Harry on the web site, asking if anyone's lost him."

"Good." Neil cheered up. At least that was something positive.

"We're going to have to do something about Harry soon," Emily said gravely.

"I know," agreed Neil. He let himself and Jake out of the field, and the Border collie immediately trotted off toward the house in search of his food bowl. "We might have to call Terri ourselves."

Emily sighed. "It's a shame. Vicky and Tom really love Harry."

"Well, maybe we should give it a day or two," Neil said thoughtfully. "Harry seems OK at the moment."

"Looks like we're going to be busy today." Emily remarked as they heard the sound of a car coming up the driveway. "Mom says she's got five boarders arriving this morning."

"I hope we get lots of visitors to the rescue center, too." Neil's eyes lit up as a young woman holding a small boy by the hand was shepherded across the courtyard by Kate Paget. The kennel assistant took them over to the rescue center, then waved at Neil and Emily.

"Hi, you two. Any news on that stray puppy?" she called.

"I saw it the other day, but wasn't in time to catch it," Neil replied. That was the truth, sort of.

"That's a shame." Kate spotted a young couple coming through the gate and hurried over to meet them.

"I hope Pirate finds a new home," Emily said to Neil.

Neil grinned. He'd just had a *brilliant* idea. "I bet he will!" he said. "Come on."

"Neil, what are you *doing*?" Emily asked impatiently as she followed him into the rescue center. The visitors were all walking up and down, looking in the pens. Pirate was standing at the front of his, wagging his stumpy tail, but no one was taking any notice.

"Good dog!" Neil said, letting himself into the pen and scratching Pirate's head affectionately. He waited until the woman and her son were walking back toward them, then took a dog treat out of his pocket. Pirate immediately sat up on his hind legs, caught the treat neatly, and took a bow.

"Mommy!" the little boy gasped. "Look at that!"

Neil grinned and repeated the trick. Meanwhile, the young couple had come over to watch, too, as well as an elderly man who'd just shown up with his granddaughter.

"Everyone's watching, Neil," Emily whispered. "Do something else."

"OK, Pirate — roll!" Neil commanded, and Pirate

neatly performed the trick, rolling first one way and then the other. The audience laughed and applauded.

"What a smart dog!" the little boy's mother said with a smile.

Neil began scratching his nose, and Pirate did the same. The audience thought this was hysterical and applauded wildly. Meanwhile, a few more visitors had turned up, and some of the people who'd dropped their dogs off at the boarding kennel had come over to see what was going on. Kate Paget had arrived, too, along with Sarah, who was munching on an apple.

"Pirate's the best!" Sarah gasped as Neil went through the repertoire of tricks once more.

"That's all, folks!" Neil took a bow, and Pirate did the same, to loud applause.

"You were fantastic, Neil," Emily laughed as the crowd began to disperse.

"No, Pirate was," Neil corrected her with a grin. "Maybe someone will realize now just what a great dog he is."

"Pirate, you're the smartest dog I've ever seen," Sarah declared, taking a huge bite of her apple. Then her face twisted in pain. *"Ow!"* Sarah spat out the bite of apple and burst into tears.

"Sarah, what is it?" Kate asked anxiously.

"My tooth!"

Kate took a quick look inside Sarah's mouth. "I think she's lost a filling," she said. "Poor little Sarah. We'd better get her to a dentist right away."

Sarah cried even harder. "*No-o-o!* I don't want to go to the dentist!"

"Come on, Squirt, it won't be so bad," Neil urged her. "Let's go and find Mom."

"Thanks for bringing us, Kate," Neil said as Kate swung her little car into the dentist's parking lot. Carole had been in the middle of an interview with some visitors at the kennel, and Bob was at the bank, so Kate had offered to drive Sarah to the dentist in Compton. Sarah had tearfully insisted that Neil go with her. She had calmed down now, though, and was sitting gloomily in the back seat.

"No problem." Kate turned off the engine. "Come on, Sarah. We'll soon get you fixed up."

Sarah climbed slowly out of the car. She clung to Neil's hand as they went into the waiting room, looking absolutely petrified.

"My tooth doesn't hurt anymore, Neil," Sarah whispered as Kate spoke to the receptionist. "We can go home now."

"It'll hurt when you eat, Squirt," Neil said gently. "Look, it won't be too bad —"

He stopped as a door opened and a woman in a white coat came into the room. It was Jo Morris. Neil just managed to stop himself from groaning. He'd forgotten that Jo was a dentist.

"Sarah Parker?" Jo said in a cool, professional voice. "Would you come in, please?"

Sarah gave a little shriek as she recognized her. "It's that horrible woman who doesn't like dogs!" she wailed.

"Sshh!" Neil could see from the frosty look on Jo's face that she'd heard every word. "It'll be OK. I'll come in with you."

"Is everything all right?" Kate was looking anxious.

"Yes, thank you," Neil said, practically dragging a reluctant Sarah into the dentist's office. Jo followed them in and shut the door.

"Now there's nothing to worry about," she said, making a visible effort to speak gently. "Sit down in the chair, please, Sarah."

Sarah stood where she was until Neil gave her a little shove. Then she climbed glumly into the chair.

"OK, Sarah, open your mouth wide." Jo Morris had pulled on some plastic gloves, and was sorting through her instruments. "Then we can take a look."

Sarah kept her mouth tightly closed, a rebellious look on her face.

"Open *wide*, please," Jo repeated more firmly.

This time, Sarah did as she was told, and the dentist began to probe her mouth. Suddenly, Sarah gave a yelp. "Ow! That hurts!" she roared, and, to Neil's dismay, she sank her teeth into the back of Jo Morris's hand.

## CHAPTER EIGHT

"**H**onestly, Sarah, how could you, sweetie?" Carole exclaimed when she heard what Sarah had done. "You bit Jo Morris!"

"But she *hurt* me," Sarah muttered miserably.

"She didn't do it on purpose, Squirt." Neil tried to be fair. "She was trying to be gentle, but you kept on moving around."

"We'll have to apologize, Bob." Carole looked as if she'd swallowed a lemon. Neil felt the same way. The idea of apologizing to Jo Morris wasn't a pleasant one.

Bob sighed. "We certainly will," he agreed. "I'd better give her a call at the dentist's office now."

"Better you than me," Carole muttered, pouring herself another cup of tea.

"Mom, were any of this morning's visitors interested in Pirate?" Neil asked eagerly.

Carole's eyes twinkled. "You could say that! Three different families are desperate to take him home!"

"Cool!" said Neil. Emily cheered, and even Sarah looked a bit happier.

"Kate told me all about your performance," Carole went on. "It obviously did the trick."

Neil grinned. It was great to know that Pirate would be going to a good home at last. "So who's the lucky new owner?" he asked.

"Well, we think he'll probably go to the Carson family," Carole replied. "Mrs. Carson has twin boys of about eleven, and a little girl of three. They live in Padsham and they seem very nice."

"And they really liked Pirate?" Neil pressed for more details.

His mom nodded. "Kate took them into the pen, and they were very impressed with how gentle Pirate was with the toddler. And I think the twins are planning to teach him a lot more tricks."

"Awesome!" Neil sat back, feeling pleased with himself. That was one problem down.

"All right, I think I'll pop into the office and finish off all that paperwork that's waiting for me." Carole sighed, beginning to clear the table.

"Have you checked the e-mails recently, Mom?" Emily asked pointedly, getting up to help.

"There was one from the Simpsons this morning, if

that's what you mean!" her mom replied. "They e-mailed pictures of some of the husky dogs."

"Oh, great!" Emily dropped the silverware she was holding into the sink and clattered off to the office.

Sarah followed her. "I think I need a vacation to get over going to the dentist," she announced, pausing in the doorway.

"Mention the word Alaska, and I'll send you straight back to Jo Morris!" her mom said cheerfully. Sarah fled.

Bob came back into the room looking grim-faced. "What did Jo Morris say now?" Neil asked.

"Oh, she was very gracious about Sarah biting her." Bob snorted. "Said it was an occupational hazard for dentists. Then she told me she was reporting King Street Kennels to the environmental health agency because of the stray dog and the dog mess on her property."

"First her lawyer, now the environmental health people — she'll be calling in the army next!" Carole said bitterly.

Neil reached under the table and patted Jake, who was sprawled out comfortably across his feet. It seemed as if relations between the Morris family and the Parkers were at an all-time low.

"Good boy, Jake!"

Neil applauded as Jake jumped neatly through the middle of the tire, then raced over the hurdles. The young dog was in top form again. Neil was relieved, but he decided to give Jake a rest for a day or two. There were still nearly two weeks to go before the competition, and Neil didn't want him to become stale.

"Neil!"

Neil turned around to see Vicky and Tom walking toward the gate, waving at him. His heart sank as he went across to meet them, Jake at his heels. They weren't going to be happy at what he had to say about Harry.

"Hi, Neil." Vicky smiled at him. "Is Jake OK after yesterday?"

"He's fine," Neil replied. "How's Harry?"

"Just great," Tom said happily. "Do you want to come and see him?"

Neil hesitated. He really did want to check up on Harry again. He remembered what his dad had said about keeping away from Old Mill Farm, but there was a dog involved. . . .

"It's OK," Tom reassured him. "Mom's at the dentist's office, and Dad's working in the trailer. The builders aren't here, either, because it's Saturday."

Neil came to a quick decision. "All right, but I can't really bring Jake. I'll have to take him home first."

Vicky and Tom waited until Neil came back, and then the three of them walked across to the farmhouse. Harry was asleep in his box when they went into the shed, but he sat up immediately, wagging his little tail when he saw Vicky and Tom. He climbed out of his bed and rushed across the shed toward them with a welcoming bark.

"Let *me* pick him up, Vicky," Tom argued, trying to elbow his sister out of the way. "It's *my* turn!"

"OK," Vicky agreed reluctantly.

Neil couldn't help smiling as Tom scooped Harry up and the puppy went crazy with delight, licking Tom's face and pressing his black nose against the boy's cheek.

"Harry looks a lot cleaner," Neil remarked. The puppy's coat was much fluffier and whiter than yesterday. "Have you given him a bath?"

"No, we didn't think that was a good idea, in case he caught a cold," Vicky said. "We just wiped him down with an old towel and some hot water."

"And we brushed him, too," Tom added.

Neil nodded approvingly. Vicky and Tom were looking after Harry really well, but that wasn't the point. They couldn't keep the puppy in the shed forever.

"It's my turn now," Vicky said impatiently, holding out her arms. Tom handed over the puppy, and Harry settled himself comfortably on Vicky's shoulder, grabbed a strand of her long blond hair, and began to chew it.

"Harry, stop it!" Vicky laughed.

"Let's show Neil Harry's favorite game," Tom suggested, picking up a rubber bone that was lying on the floor. Vicky put Harry down, and Tom held out the bone to him.

"Come on, Harry," Tom urged him. "Good dog!"

Harry launched himself at the bone with a playful little growl, then clung on to it with his teeth. Tom pulled the other end hard, but Harry hung on and refused to let go.

"Isn't he cute?" Vicky smiled.

Neil was beginning to feel very uncomfortable. It was obvious that Vicky and Tom were becoming very attached to Harry and were going to find it difficult to give him up. The longer they looked after him, the worse it would be.

*It's now or never*, Neil thought. "Have you told your mom about Harry yet?"

"We'll tell her soon," Vicky muttered, her face falling.

"When?" Neil knew he had to push the issue, for Harry's sake.

"Tomorrow," Tom said quickly.

Vicky saw the look on Neil's face. "Mom'll like Harry, Neil. You don't know her like we do. She *loves* animals."

*Except dogs.* The unspoken words hung in the air between them.

"All right," Neil said reluctantly. "One more day. But that's all."

Harry had dropped the bone now, and was yawning widely. He padded over to his bed, climbed in, and curled up into a little furry ball. In a moment or two, he was fast asleep again.

"He gets tired really quickly," Tom said.

"Well, puppies do sleep a lot," Neil replied. "But Harry's not as strong as he should be. That's why he needs to see a vet — and soon."

"We wanted to ask you a favor, actually." Vicky changed the subject quickly. "We're all going to visit our grandma tomorrow, and we wondered if you and Emily would keep an eye on Harry for us. I'll leave his food in the shed, and the builders won't be here because it's Sunday."

"OK," he agreed.

"Thanks, Neil," Vicky said gratefully. "We'll tell

Mom about Harry as soon as we get back from Gran's."

Neil felt like saying that they might as well not bother. There was no way they'd be keeping Harry. But Vicky and Tom obviously loved the little dog, and one more day wouldn't make much difference. . . .

## CHAPTER NINE

"**A**re you and Jake coming to the obedience class, Neil?" Bob pushed his empty cereal bowl away and stood up.

"Not today, Dad," Neil glanced at Emily. He'd told her about Vicky's and Tom's request yesterday, and his sister was up for it. "I want to give Jake a complete break from any kind of training for a few days."

"Good idea." Bob picked up his jacket. "You want to make sure he stays fresh."

"Mom, I need to clean out Fudge's cage," Sarah said. "Will you help me?"

Carole sighed. "What a wonderful job for a Sunday morning! All right, let's get on with it."

Neil and Emily waited impatiently until the kitchen was empty, and then leaped up from their chairs. As Emily opened the back door, Jake padded out from under the table and looked hopefully at Neil, who shook his head.

"Not this time, boy," he said. Jake slumped down, head on his paws, and gloomily watched them leave.

"Do you really think Vicky and Tom will tell their mom about Harry today?" Emily asked as they walked toward the deserted farmhouse.

"I don't know," Neil replied. "But I'm calling Terri McCall first thing tomorrow anyway."

The puppy was nowhere to be seen when they walked into the shed. Emily hurried over to check his bed while Neil did his best to push the rickety old door shut. As Emily bent over the cardboard box, she gave a gasp of horror.

"Neil!" she cried. "Come here! *Quick!*"

Neil rushed over immediately and looked into the box. Harry laid with his nose on his paws, breathing shallowly, eyes closed. He looked listless and ill, and the food Vicky and Tom had put down that morning hadn't been touched.

"What's wrong with him?" Emily asked fearfully.

"I don't know." Neil stroked Harry's head gently. He blamed himself now for not insisting that Vicky and Tom hand Harry over to the ASPCA right away. This was the result.

Harry opened his eyes and began to wag his tail feebly. Then he gave a dry, hacking cough that shook his whole body.

Emily glanced at Neil. "That sounds like —"

"Kennel cough," Neil finished grimly.

As Harry coughed again, his little body trembling, Neil tried desperately to remember what he knew about the infectious disease. It usually wasn't too serious, and a dose of cough medicine and sometimes antibiotics could be all that was needed to cure it. But Neil remembered Mike Turner saying that it could be more serious if the dog had recently been under a lot of stress — in some cases, it could even lead to pneumonia.

"He's going to be all right, isn't he, Neil?" Emily asked shakily.

"I don't know. Harry's weak and undernourished, and he might have other infections that we don't know about yet." Neil forced himself to think clearly. What was the best thing to do?

"We'll have to take Harry back to King Street," he said slowly. "You go ahead, Em, and warn Dad, so we can make sure all the dogs are safely shut away. Then there's no risk of infection. We'll have to get Harry to Mike Turner as fast as we can."

"OK." Emily nodded, her face pale. "Should I go right now?"

"Yes." Neil pulled off his sweatshirt and gently wrapped Harry in it. "I'll come after you, in about ten minutes —"

"I thought I heard voices! What are you two doing in here?"

Jo Morris was standing in the doorway, staring at them.

Neil almost jumped out of his skin. He'd been so worried about Harry, he hadn't heard a thing. Neither had Emily, from the look on her face. Neil certainly hadn't expected anyone to be around — Vicky had said that the whole family was going to visit her grandmother.

"I said, what's going on?" Jo Morris asked, crossing the shed toward them. Then she spotted the bundled-up sweatshirt in Neil's arms, with the little furry head poking out of it, and her eyes widened. "What's *that*?"

Neil hugged Harry closer. "It's the stray puppy," he explained abruptly. "Vicky and Tom have been looking after him for the last few days. They asked Em and me to check on him today, but he's sick. We're taking him back to King Street so Dad can drive us to the vet's."

Jo Morris's mouth fell open. She seemed to be lost for words. "V-Vicky and Tom have been looking after a puppy — *here*?" she stammered.

"They wanted to keep him," Neil added, unable to keep a note of sarcasm out of his voice.

Jo Morris seemed to have lost the power of speech. She stared at Harry as if she were in a daze, then jumped as the puppy suddenly had another coughing fit.

"I'd better go, Neil," Emily said urgently, hurrying over to the door.

Jo Morris was still staring at the sick puppy.

"What's the matter with him?"

"Kennel cough," Neil replied. "It's not usually that serious, but Harry's not in the best condition to fight off any infection."

"Harry?" Jo Morris frowned. "Is that what Vicky and Tom named him?"

"I'll be going now, Neil." Emily was still hovering in the doorway.

"No, wait," Jo said decisively. She looked at Neil. "I'll drive you to the vet's."

"What?" Neil wondered if he'd heard right.

"I'll drive you myself," Jo repeated crisply. "It'll save time. Besides, if Vicky and Tom have been keeping this puppy here, I suppose that makes it my responsibility — for the moment, anyway."

"All right," Neil agreed. He still didn't like Jo Morris, but it would mean that Harry got proper medical attention more quickly. "Em, you run home and tell Mom and Dad what's happened." Then he turned to Jo Morris. "I'll have to call Mike Turner at his house and get him to meet us at the clinic."

"All right, Neil, I've got him." Mike Turner gently took the puppy bundled up in the sweatshirt and unwrapped him like a very precious package. Neil watched anxiously, with Jo Morris standing at his side. They had driven into Compton without speaking, the silence broken only by Harry's pitiful coughs.

Neil had seen Jo glance sideways at the puppy, but he hadn't been able to guess what she was thinking.

"What do you think?" Neil asked impatiently as Mike made a quick initial examination of Harry. The puppy was still coughing hard, his little body racked with pain.

"It doesn't look good, Neil," the vet said quietly. "He's very weak. He's obviously been sick for some time."

Neil swallowed a lump in his throat. Jo Morris looked shocked, too.

"He's not going to *die*?" Jo exclaimed. Then she flushed as Neil glanced at her. "Vicky and Tom would be very upset," she added quickly.

"I'm going to examine him thoroughly and run some tests, then we'll have a better idea." The vet nodded toward the waiting room. "Go and take a seat, OK?"

"You don't have to wait," Neil said as he and Jo left the examining room and sat down.

Jo shrugged. "Vicky and Tom will want to know how the puppy is," she muttered.

They sat in uncomfortable silence for a few minutes.

"My parents didn't know about any of this," Neil felt obliged to say. "Em and I only came to look after Harry because Vicky and Tom asked us to — they said there'd be nobody at home."

"Well, I was supposed to be going, too, but I de-

cided to stay at home and work on the campaign —"
Jo began. Then she flushed a deep red.

"Spread some more lies about King Street Kennels, you mean," Neil said bitterly. He thought Jo
might take offense at that, but she didn't. Instead
she stared at him thoughtfully.

"You love dogs, don't you, Neil?"

"Yes," Neil said defiantly. "And you don't, obviously." He stared back at Jo. "What have you got
against them?" He thought there would never be a
better time than this to try to find out.

"I was attacked by a friend's dog when I was only
three," Jo said abruptly. "I was very badly bitten and
had to have a lot of painful surgery." She tried to
keep her voice steady, but didn't quite manage it.

Neil could see that she was still deeply affected by
the incident, even after all these years. "I'm sorry. I
didn't know," he said quietly.

"My mother saw the whole thing," Jo went on. "So,
of course, after that, she was terrified of dogs, too. We
were both hysterical with fear if we even *saw* a dog."
She laughed shortly. "Seems silly, doesn't it, when
you look at a tiny little thing like Harry?"

Just then, Mike Turner opened the door and beckoned them back into his examining room. Neil jumped
up quickly, his mind going over what Jo Morris had
said. He was beginning to understand why she had
behaved the way she had, but he still didn't like it.

"How is he, Mike?" Neil asked anxiously, staring

down at Harry, who lay on his side on the examining table.

The vet smiled. "It's OK, Neil. He's not quite as bad as I thought. He's a tough little fellow!"

Neil gave a huge sigh of relief. He glanced at Jo, but she said nothing.

"But Harry *is* quite weak because he hasn't been eating properly for some time, and the kennel cough's not helping," Mike went on. "I've given him a shot of antibiotics, which should help to clear up the cough."

"So what happens now?" Neil asked.

"Well, Harry doesn't really need specialized care. He just needs to be kept warm, fed light, nourishing food at regular intervals, and given regular doses of cough medicine and antibiotics." Mike turned to Jo. "How do you feel about nursing Harry yourself, Mrs. Morris?"

"*What?*" Jo gasped.

"Well, your family has been caring for Harry for the last few days, haven't they?" Mike asked, puzzled.

"Um . . . no, not exactly," Jo said, looking flustered.

"Oh, I see." Mike frowned. "The problem is, Harry's got to be isolated from other dogs, and I haven't got room for him here at the moment."

"What about the animal hospital in Padsham?" suggested Neil.

"Their isolation wing's full," said Mike. "I might be able to get him into the big hospital in Wingfield, but that's on the other side of the county. It's a long way for a sick puppy to travel."

Neil stared hard at Jo Morris. *This is your chance to make up for your campaign against King Street Kennels,* he urged her silently. *Come on!*

"Well . . ." Jo Morris muttered uncomfortably. "I suppose Vicky and Tom would never forgive me if I didn't say yes."

# CHAPTER TEN

**"D**o you think he'll be warm enough there?" Jo asked anxiously as Neil placed the cardboard box in front of the trailer's heater and put Harry gently inside.

"He'll be fine," Neil replied. He could still hardly believe that Jo had agreed to take Harry home. "Have you got that list Mike gave us?"

Jo pulled it out of her handbag. "Yes, it says when to give him his pills, and lists the kinds of food he should be eating."

"And Mike said to give him the cough medicine whenever he needs it," Neil reminded her.

"I'll tape this list up on the refrigerator so I don't lose it." Jo went into the tiny kitchen at the back of the trailer and made a face. "Sorry about the mess."

The trailer *was* pretty cramped, Neil thought, especially for four people. It had a living room, two bedrooms, a kitchen, and a bathroom, but all the rooms were tiny and full of boxes and bags.

Harry had struggled to his feet and was standing, sniffing the air. That was a good sign, Neil thought. It meant the antibiotics were starting to work.

"What's the matter with him?" Jo asked, alarmed, as Harry began scratching the side of the box.

"I think he wants to come out for a bit," Neil lifted the puppy up and Harry snuggled in his lap, rubbing his head against Neil's hand.

"He must be feeling a bit better," Jo said hopefully.

"Why don't you hold him?" Neil asked.

"Oh!" Jo looked startled. "I don't think I could. . . ."

"If you're going to look after him, you'll have to," Neil pointed out, and before Jo could say anything else, he put Harry into her arms.

Jo trembled as Harry sniffed at her fingers and then settled down on her lap for a nap. "You know, this is the first dog I've touched in about thirty years!" she said in a shaky voice, stroking Harry's soft head gingerly. "Isn't that silly?"

"Well, I hope it's not the last!" Neil said with a grin.

The sound of a car outside the trailer made them both look up. The next moment the door flew open.

"Hi, Mom!" Tom rushed into the trailer followed by Vicky. "Gran was really sorry you didn't come —" He stopped dead in his tracks when he saw Harry lying asleep in his mother's arms, and Vicky crashed right into him.

"Mom! That's Harry!" Tom stammered. Vicky was too dumbfounded to say anything.

"Who's Harry?" Graham Morris followed them into the trailer, looking puzzled. Then his mouth fell open in amazement as he saw his wife holding the sleeping puppy.

Jo glanced at Neil. "It's a long story," she said.

\*     \*     \*

"I still can't believe Jo Morris said she'd look after the puppy!" Carole remarked. "Maybe she's not as bad as we thought she was."

"I'm not sure she'll let Vicky and Tom keep him," Neil said thoughtfully, "but I don't think she'll be quite so scared of dogs anymore."

It was later that evening, and the Parkers had just finished their dinner. Neil was wondering whether to drop by Old Mill Farm to see how Harry was, but he wasn't sure how welcoming Jo Morris would be. She might even be regretting her decision to take Harry home.

"I suppose you can't blame her after what happened to her," Bob said thoughtfully as he stacked the dirty plates. "It must have been a terrible experience."

"Dad, do you think she'll drop the campaign against our kennel now?" Emily asked.

Bob shrugged. "Who knows? We'd better not get our hopes up."

Just then, the doorbell rang. Neil slid out of his seat.

"I'll get it."

He went down the hall, Jake padding along after him, and opened the door. Jo Morris was standing outside.

"Oh, hello, Neil," she said with a nervous smile. "Are your mom and dad in?"

Neil nodded warily. He still didn't really trust her after everything that had happened. Silently, he showed her into the kitchen. Bob, Carole, and Emily looked very surprised to see her, and Sarah turned bright red.

"I'll get straight to the point, Mr. and Mrs. Parker," Jo said frankly. "I feel we got off on the wrong foot when we moved here, and . . ." her voice faltered, "a lot of that was my fault. I want to apologize."

Neil was stunned. He glanced at his father, who looked equally shocked.

"How about if we forget all about it and start again?" Bob said quietly, offering Jo his hand.

Jo shook it hesitantly. "That's very good of you, Mr. Parker."

"Bob, please," he told her.

"And Carole," Neil's mom added.

"Well, I just wanted to let you know that I'm dropping the campaign," Jo muttered. She smiled ruefully. "I never got much support for it, anyway."

"We're very glad to hear it!" Carole said as Neil sighed with relief. "And I think Sarah's got something she'd like to say." She glanced at her youngest daughter.

"I'm sorry I bit you, Mrs. Morris," Sarah mumbled.

"That's OK, Sarah." Jo shrugged. "It's happened to me before, and it'll probably happen again."

"How's Harry?" Neil asked eagerly.

"Oh, just one day has made a big difference," Jo exclaimed, brightening up. "The cough's not so bad, and he's already looking better. The vet's coming to see him tonight."

"Great," Neil said, grinning at Jo's enthusiasm. She actually sounded pleased!

"Well, I'd better go," Jo said awkwardly. "You and Emily are welcome to visit Harry anytime you like, Neil."

"Thanks." Neil couldn't help wondering if there was a faint chance that Vicky and Tom would get to keep Harry after all. He would just have to wait and see. . . .

"Hi, you two!" Vicky flung open the trailer door and beamed at Neil and Emily. "Come in!"

"And watch out for Harry," Tom called. "He keeps trying to get out!"

Right on cue, Harry scrambled across the trailer's floor, his little tail wagging frantically, and leaped up at Neil's legs. Neil laughed and bent down to pet him. He could hardly believe that this lively, sturdy pup was the same sick, listless dog of just over a week ago. Harry had recovered fast and was now almost back to normal weight, plus his kennel cough had completely disappeared.

"Tom, you're not tiring Harry out, are you?" Jo called anxiously from the kitchen. She looked embarrassed when she saw Neil and Emily. "Oh . . . hello, you two."

"Come in and sit down," called Graham Morris, who was working at his computer on the small pull-down table. "If you can find a space!"

Neil and Emily squeezed into the living room past all the boxes and bags. Harry followed them, sniffing at Neil's sneakers, grabbing the laces in his teeth and hanging on as Neil tried to walk across the trailer.

"How's Jake's training going, Neil?" Tom asked.

"OK," Neil said. "Are you coming to the county show next week? It's only Padsham. Then you can watch Jake in the agility competition."

"Can we, Mom?" Vicky asked eagerly.

Jo smiled. "I don't see why not. Would you and Emily like a drink, Neil?"

"No, we can't stay long," Neil said. "We just came to tell you that Terri McCall phoned Dad this morning about Harry."

Vicky and Tom looked shocked, and so did their dad. Even Jo looked alarmed.

"Did she find Harry's owner?" Vicky asked anxiously.

Neil shook his head, looking at Jo. She was obviously trying hard not to show any emotion, although the rest of her family gasped with relief.

"No one's come forward to claim him," Emily said. "And Mike says he's not microchipped, so there's no way of finding the owner."

"So, as soon as he's healthy enough, Harry can come to the rescue center and go up for adoption," Neil added.

Vicky and Tom immediately turned to Jo.

"*Mom!*" they both said pleadingly.

"We'll talk about this later." Jo shook her head warningly, and went back into the kitchen. Harry bounced after her, skidding on the polished floor, and began to tug at the leg of her jeans with his teeth.

"Harry!" Jo muttered, trying to pull away, but she was smiling. Neil's hopes rose again. Maybe Harry wouldn't need to find a new home after all. . . .

"OK, Jake, it's up to you now!" Neil muttered as he released his hold on the young dog's collar. He'd walked the agility course twice in the blazing heat.

It was a difficult course, but many of the other dogs had managed clear rounds. Jake and Neil were the last team in the junior category of the competition, so Neil knew exactly what he was up against.

"Go, Jake!" Neil shouted, and the Border collie shot off confidently toward the first jump. Neil followed, his heart thudding with nerves. But he soon calmed down as Jake cleared the first jump easily and raced toward the bridge and the first yellow contact point.

"Down!" Neil yelled, and Jake dropped like a stone onto his belly, waiting for Neil to give the signal to move on again. They moved around the course — over the bridge and down the other side, through the rigid tunnel, over the jumps, and through the tire. Jake didn't put a foot in the wrong place or miss a single contact point. Neil was barely aware of the large crowd, including his own family, who were all watching intently from behind the barriers. Nor was he conscious of the county fair, which was in full swing around him. He was completely focused on Jake and the obstacles they had to tackle.

As Jake touched the last contact point, cleared the last jump, and raced toward the finish line, Neil punched the air in delight. A clear round and no penalty points! It was even more than he was hoping for — after all, it was Jake's first competition. But was it fast enough? Breathing hard, Neil waited for

Jake's time to be announced. Even second or third place would be a great start.

"Well done, Jake!" The announcer's voice crackled over the loudspeaker. "That's the fastest time of all our competitors today! Which means that Samsboy Puppy Patrol Jake is —"

"The winner!" Neil yelled, throwing his arms around Jake's neck. The collie barked proudly, rubbing his head against Neil's. "Jake, you won!"

"Wow! You were both amazing!" Emily rushed over to them, followed by the rest of the Parker family. To Neil's surprise, the Morrises were there, too.

"Good work, son," Bob said, as Carole gave Neil a hug and Sarah wrapped her arms around Jake.

"Yes, you were great, Neil," Tom added. He was holding Harry on a leash, and the little pup was jumping around excitedly, looking fully recovered from his illness. He'd had his injections now and was obviously enjoying being surrounded by all sorts of other dogs.

"Very impressive, Neil." Jo Morris gave him a friendly smile. "And you, too, Jake."

Jake heard his name and wagged his tail, leaning over to sniff Jo's hand. Jo flinched, but she managed to pat Jake timidly on the head.

"Harry's jealous, Mom," Vicky said teasingly as the puppy pulled Tom toward Jo. "You know how much he likes you."

"Don't be silly, Vicky!" Jo said quickly, but Neil thought she looked quite pleased.

Meanwhile, Jake and Harry were sniffing at each other cautiously. Harry seemed very impressed by the older dog — so much so that he began to run around wildly in circles, trying to catch his own tail, and ended up getting tangled up in his leash. Everyone laughed.

"Oh, Harry!" Jo smiled, shaking her head as she bent down to free him.

"Maybe Harry will be able to take part in agility competitions when he's older," Tom said. "Will you help us to teach him, Neil?"

Neil's heart lurched. "You mean you're keeping him?"

"Yes!" Vicky said firmly, glancing at her mother.

"Vicky!" Jo said, flustered. "Nothing's been decided yet."

"But we all love him, Mom!" Vicky said urgently.

"Yes, we do," Tom backed her up. "Don't we, Dad?"

Graham looked at his wife. "He's a great little dog, honey."

Jo glanced down at Harry, who was now blissfully chewing the bottoms of her pants. "Well . . ." She rolled her eyes. "I must be crazy! As if we haven't got enough problems already with the house renovations and living in a trailer!"

"Oh, thanks, Mom!" Vicky and Tom squealed, and

they launched themselves at Jo. Neil grinned. The day was turning out even better than he'd hoped.

"It's time for the ribbon ceremony." Emily nudged Neil as the winners of the various classes began to assemble in the arena. "The Hammonds are going to be pleased when they hear that Jake won."

"Well, you'll be able to tell them in person when you go to New York," Carole said casually, and then laughed as Neil and Emily did a double take.

"You mean we're going to America after all?" Neil gasped. "Will we get to see Max and Prince in Hollywood?"

"And the Simpsons in Alaska?" Emily asked.

Bob grinned. "We haven't worked out all the details yet, but we thought maybe Neil and Emily could go and stay with the Hammonds in New York, and then move on to Hollywood to see Max and Prince —"

"What, on our *own*?" Emily asked, shooting an ecstatic look at Neil.

Carole nodded. "We think you're mature enough — just barely!" she said teasingly. "Then we'll fly over a bit later with Sarah, and we'll all meet up in Alaska to see the Simpsons. How does that sound?"

"Fantastic —" Neil began, just as a voice over the loudspeaker announced, *"Neil Parker and Jake, please join the winners in the arena. The ribbon ceremony is about to start."*

"Come on, Jake," Neil murmured. Today was like a dream come true. He was going to America, Jo Morris had accepted Harry, Pirate had a new home, and Jake had won his first agility competition.

But as a smiling judge pinned a gold *1st Prize* ribbon to Jake's collar, Neil knew that he wasn't dreaming.

*Jake did it, Sam,* he thought. *You'd be as proud of your son as I am!*